# RODDY DOYLE

Roddy Doyle was born in Dublin in 1958. He is the author of twelve acclaimed novels including *The Commitments*, *The Snapper*, *The Van* and *Smile*, three collections of short stories, and *Rory & Ita,* a memoir about his parents. He won the Booker Prize in 1993 for *Paddy Clarke Ha Ha Ha*.

RODDY DOYLE

# Life Without Children

## Stories

**VINTAGE**

3 5 7 9 10 8 6 4

Vintage is part of the Penguin Random House group of companies
whose addresses can be found at global.penguinrandomhouse.com

Penguin
Random House
UK

'Box Sets' 'The Curfew' and 'Life Without Children' first appeared in the
New Yorker; 'Nurse' first appeared in the Irish Times.

Lyrics: 'Strawberry Fields Forever', Songwriters: John Lennon and
Paul McCartney; 'Gypsy Rover (The Whistling Gypsy)', Songwriter:
Leo Maguire; 'I'm Not in Love', Songwriters: Eric Stewart and Graham
Gouldman; 'I Will Survive', Songwriters: Freddie Perren and Dino
Fekaris; 'Midnight Train to Georgia', Songwriter: Jim Weatherly

First published in Vintage in 2022
First published in hardback by Jonathan Cape in 2021

penguin.co.uk/vintage

A CIP catalogue record for this book is available from the British Library

ISBN 9781529115024

Printed and bound in Great Britain by Clays Ltd, Elcograf S.p.A.

The authorised representative in the EEA is Penguin Random House Ireland,
Morrison Chambers, 32 Nassau Street, Dublin D02 YH68

Penguin Random House is committed to a sustainable future
for our business, our readers and our planet. This book is made
from Forest Stewardship Council® certified paper.

MIX
Paper from
responsible sources
FSC® C018179

'It's only the bleedin' flu'

The man in SuperValu

# Contents

1. Box Sets   1
2. The Curfew   15
3. Life Without Children   29
4. Gone   43
5. Nurse   66
6. Masks   70
7. The Charger   76
8. The Funeral   115
9. Worms   128
10. The Five Lamps   149

# Box Sets

There'd nearly been a fight. People were drinking wine like it was beer and a man Sam didn't know had thumped the table and shouted that *House of Cards* was better than *Breaking Bad* and *Mad Men*, put together.

—All the seasons!

The man had knocked over a glass.

A woman had thrown a fist-load of peanuts at him, although most of them bounced off the table. She seemed to be defending *Breaking Bad* and *Mad Men*. Sam wasn't sure. He hadn't seen either. His wife, Emer, had been in the middle of it, too, standing up for *The Killing*, the Danish version. Sam hadn't seen *The Killing* and he hadn't a clue how Emer had managed it.

They'd walked home, staggering a bit.

—When did you watch *The Killing*?

—I didn't.

—It seemed like you did.

—Yeah, well, I didn't. But, like, everyone says it's brilliant.

He'd watched it since. Seasons One, Two and Three. And it *was* brilliant. He'd watched *The Bridge* too. And *Love/Hate*. And a good chunk of *The Wire*. They were all great.

But he'd felt late getting to them. Too late, and too slow. He knew that if the same people were to meet around a table now they'd be getting worked up about a whole new bunch of box sets, or something new on Netflix, and he'd be lost again.

He'd watched *The Killing* alone while Emer was at work. He'd watched most of Season One in a day. It was mesmerising. He'd been going to buy Emer one of the striped jumpers the detective, Sarah Lund, wore. But he'd done a search – €310, for a genuine one from the Faroe Islands. There was no way he was spending that kind of money, not now.

He didn't have a job. That still felt like a smack, three months later. Just when they'd both begun to think they'd survived the worst of it, when they were starting to hear and believe the optimism on the radio. *We're seeing light at the end of the tunnel. This is great news for Ireland Inc.* He'd been called in for a chat.

He'd started sending out the CVs the day after he came home jobless. He'd signed up with an agency. He'd even ticked the box that let them know he was prepared to go to the UK, Australia or Canada. It would be temporary. It could be exciting. He hadn't hesitated.

But nothing.

He was too slow, again. Too late. One of the banks was advertising mortgages for people who were thinking of coming back home to Ireland, from the UK, Australia and Canada.

They'd be fine. Emer said it, and they said it together. They touched glasses and smiled. They'd tighten the belts, just a bit. They'd renegotiate the mortgage, but only when they had to. They'd stretch the six remaining years to twelve, or fifteen.

2

—We'll drink less.

—No way.

They laughed. She patted the dog on her lap.

—And we'll feed you a bit less, Chester, she said. —Cos you're a fat little fucker, aren't you.

He wasn't fat – the dog. Neither was Sam.

Just when they'd thought they were safe. They hadn't been alone in thinking that. The cookbooks were a sign of the shift. Whenever they went to people's houses – and they did it a lot, on Friday and Saturday evenings, the homes of people Emer knew from work or old friends she'd kept in touch with – they were given food that was supposedly eaten on the streets of cities that Sam associated with bombings or destitution. Beirut street food, Mumbai street food. Jerusalem was the latest – Ottolenghi. The recipe book was always on the kitchen counter, and they'd have to hear the tale of the hunt for the ingredients before they were allowed to eat.

Not that he objected to the food. He cooked a bit himself. Dublin street food, and the odd Mexican or Far Eastern dish. But, anyway, that was the start of the country's comeback, he'd thought. And Emer had agreed with him. The street food books – the money to buy them and the money to use them, the tiny bit of ostentation. The books alone on the counter, and the box sets piled beside the telly. One night, he'd even made up a story about a couple on the Southside who'd served up barbequed fox – medieval street food. He'd added a joust in the back garden and an outbreak of cholera before everyone around the table realised that he was joking.

That was the last time he'd been funny.

Something had snapped, or sagged, a few weeks after he was let go. Someone sitting beside him at a different dinner, someone else he didn't know, had asked him what he did and he hadn't been able to answer. Not a word.

The next time Emer had told him they were going to someone's house on a Friday he'd said No.

—What?

She hadn't looked at him yet. She was just in from work, concentrating on the dog.

—I'd prefer not to, Sam said.

He hated the sound of that, the voice and the words, the pompous little boy. But he'd said it.

—Why not? she asked.

She was sitting on the kitchen floor, shoving the dog across the tiles and enjoying his return. She looked up at Sam.

—Ah, said Sam. —I don't –. I just –

—What?

—Why is it always your decision?

—Hang on, she said. —What?

She was standing now, taking her coat off.

—What did you say? she asked. —I mean, what do you mean?

She smiled.

—Well, he said. —Why is it like that?

—Sorry – like what?

—You come home and announce we're going to Fifi's house –

—Fiona's.

—Grand. Sorry. But you never ask.

—Ask what?

—If, like. If I want to go – or if we should go.

—What's wrong?

—Nothing's wrong.

—There's something wrong.

—There isn't.

—Is it the job?

—No, it's not the fuckin' job.

—Sam.

—What?

—Just stop it.

—Stop what?

—Ah, Sam, she said. —Listen.

She was moving again, across the kitchen. She was brilliant at this, making normality out of the tension. She put the kettle under the tap.

—Sam, she said.

—Don't patronise me, Sam said.

—I'm talking to you.

—Okay.

—I know what you're going through. Don't say anything –. I know it must be terrible – okay? But you'll get another job, wait and see. You're highly skilled.

He let her go on.

—This is temporary, she said.

She tossed a teabag into a mug.

—Agreed? Sam?

—Okay, he said.

—You think that too, I know. You know. It's temporary.

—Yeah, he said.

—So, she said. —We keep on going. Business as usual.

She was working the top off the mocha pot now, making him coffee. He didn't drink tea.

—I suppose so, he said. —But it's been three months.

—That's nothing, she said. —We've both heard about people who were waiting for years.

But it wasn't about the job, or any job, or how he'd spend the time.

—It's just – like –.

—What? she said.

She smiled. It amazed him, how she managed this. It never looked frozen or insincere. She loved him. Her tea was in her hands, his coffee was on the gas.

—All these invitations, he said.

—They're not invitations, she said back. —It's not formal. They're, like. Just, people – friends.

—Yeah, but your friends. I know no one.

—You do.

—Not really.

—Come on, Sam. They're our friends.

—Some of them, he said.

—Is that not enough?

The pot was bubbling. He took a mug from the shelf. He took the pot off the gas.

—Thanks, he said.

—No worries.

He sipped the coffee, and gave her the thumbs-up.

—Why don't you volunteer? she said.

—What?

—Do stuff, she said. —You know. Meet people.

—People?

—Stop it, Sam. You know what people are. Everybody's volunteering these days.

—I don't want to fuckin' volunteer, he said.

—Why not? What's wrong? I'm worried about you, Sam – really. I am.

He said nothing – he couldn't think of anything. He didn't want the coffee; he could feel it burning his gut.

—It'll give a shape to your day, she said. —Sam?

—Listen, he said. —Emer.

—Go on.

She looked so eager, so ready to help.

He threw the mug.


He walked ahead as the dog ran back for the ball. He walked into the wind and the bit of rain. It wasn't dark yet. The sun was a lump sinking behind the city.

He'd apologised to Emer, and said he'd bring the dog for a walk, get some air. He couldn't look at her. He'd found the dog's ball and lead in the drawer under the sink, and he'd left. He'd called Bye from the front door but she hadn't answered.

The dog was back. He dropped the ball in front of Sam.

—Good man.

It bounced, and rolled off the path onto the grass. Sam moved to pick it up.

And it happened.

A guy on a bike went into him. But Sam didn't know that. All he knew was the pain.

He was on the ground by the time what had happened began to assemble itself. He saw the bike, and the guy sprawled on the path a bit further away. He heard a noise he didn't recognise. It took a while to know that he was making it. Grunting, blowing, pushing back the pain. He could hear the skid now, the sound of the guy pulling the brake. He heard the guy's protest.

—Get out of the way!

Now he heard the guy groaning, and a wave hitting the other side of the sea wall. He heard himself. Breathing like he'd been running for hours, shoving the air out. Bellowing. He didn't know if he could move.

There was no one else around. Normally, this time of day, there'd be other people walking their dogs, or running, or even the homeless lads looking for somewhere to hide for the night. But there was no one.

He moved a leg – he could. He rolled to his side. He lifted himself. Jesus though, God. Jesus, the pain. He kept going. He felt huge. He stood up out of the wet and the injustice; that was how he felt, how he saw himself. Made monstrous.

The guy was sitting, rolling his shoulder, bleeding from his mouth. Sam roared over to the bike. That was what it was, what it felt like. Roaring, not walking. He was noise. He got across to the bike. He picked it up – it had no weight – and he threw it over the low wall, into the sea. He didn't look at the guy. The Lycra fucker. He said nothing to him and he heard nothing.

Anger got him home. Blind fury got him home. He shouldn't have been able to do it. It was usually a ten-minute walk. But he didn't know how long it took. He'd no memory of it, after. He got back up the hill. To the house. He met no one.

He got to the gate, and the door. He fell into the hall. He lay there. The pain was new – the shock was outrageous. The charge home had been an interruption. He fell to the rug and it started all over again.

Emer was there.

So was her suitcase. Right at his head, where he'd landed. She pushed it, wheeled it, out of their way. But it was there, behind her as she got down on her knees beside him.

—What happened?

He roared again now. There was a ceiling over him. The front door was closed.

—Sam?

He roared once more.

—What happened you?

—The dog.

She looked for bite marks. She searched him for blood.

—I left the dog.

It made no sense. What he'd said to Emer. He knew that.

She was wearing her coat.

—The dog, he said again.

The words hurt. Just speaking. They were followed by a groan, a yelp.

—I'll find him, she said.

She understood. But she stayed where she was. She put her hands on his chest.

—What happened?

—He went right into my back.

—The dog?

He was afraid to gasp properly. The effort shook his ribs. They were broken. They had to be.

—Bike, he said. —Prick on a bike.

—God.

—He went right into me.

—God.

—Sorry, he said.

The anger was gone and the real pain was climbing out of him.

—Can you move your legs? Emer asked.

—Think so.

He didn't remind her that he'd just walked up from the seafront. He'd do whatever she told him to.

—Okay, she said. —Carefully. Move your left leg. Lift it.

He did.

—Slowly, she said. —That's great. Down, slowly. Now the right.

—The dog.

—He'll be grand. Okay. Your spine's not broken anyway.

—Jesus.

He was breathing through his mouth. He couldn't close it.

—Lift your arm.

He lifted his right hand. She held it, helped him. The pain – something was ripping, already ripped.

—Oh Jesus, oh Jesus –!

She brought his hand back down to the rug.

—The other one. Sam?

—What?

—Your other hand.

It was bad. Bad – but not as bad.

—Good, she said. —Can you lie on your side?

She got him to bed. She held his elbow and stayed a step below him on the stairs. She had to cut his jumper off him; he couldn't lift his arms. She stood behind him with the scissors. She sliced from the bottom up, to his neck. She came back around and pulled the sleeves off his arms. She watched as he lowered himself onto the bed. He groaned, he puffed – he couldn't lie back. She got pillows from elsewhere, and came back. She piled them until he could sit and let go.

—Thanks.


He was alone. She'd gone. He heard her on the stairs. He heard the bell. He heard the front door – she was opening it. He heard a voice, a man's. A taxi driver? It wasn't a conversation – it was too short. The door closed. He heard her boots on the path outside. He couldn't hear the wheels of her case.

He couldn't move. He could, but it was awful. More minutes of gasping. He didn't know what to do. He was stuck and the house was empty. He'd never sleep.


She woke him. It was dark.

—Sam?

She was still wearing her coat. She'd been out in the cold; he could smell it.

—Hi.

He hadn't moved. He was still sitting back, against all of the house's pillows.

—I found Chester, she said.

—Great.

Talking, that one word, rubbed against the pain. He sucked in.

—Alright?

—Yeah, he said. —Where was he?

—Down where you left him.

—Okay.

—He was fine.

—Okay.

—There was no sign of the cyclist.

—Okay.

—Or the bike.

He said nothing.

She was gone again.


He woke. She wasn't in the bed. It was still dark. He'd no idea what time it was. He couldn't read his watch and he couldn't move, shift, to see the clock on the table just behind his head.

He'd been so angry when he'd left the house. He'd dragged the anger down the street with the dog, and along the seafront. He'd left behind a smashed mug and a crying woman.

—I'm leaving, she'd said while he was putting the lead on the dog.

He'd thrown the mug at the wall, above the cooker.

—Don't let me stop you, he'd said, looking at the dog's neck.

He was an idiot.

Emer was right; they'd be fine. They'd have to be – *he'd* have to be.

He could hear nothing in the house.

He had to go to the toilet. He had to move. He turned, kind of rolled to his right. He pulled back the yell, sucked it back down. He didn't want to hear it. He sent his feet out. The right one touched the floor. He rolled again. He was off the bed, on his knees – a little kid saying his prayers. He straightened his back. Christ, Jesus. He stood up.

He walked out to the landing. He leaned on the wall, and the door frame. Across to the bathroom. He had to bend, to lift the seat. Christ, Christ. He pissed, he flushed. Back out to the landing. He could hear nothing else, just himself, just his breath. She might have been in one of the other bedrooms. He went back across to their room.

He stopped. He turned – the change of direction stabbed him. He went for the stairs. The drop to the hall looked deep and dark. Each step was agony. No, sore. Just sore. Very sore. He made it to the bottom. Her case was gone, not in the hall. He got to the kitchen. There was sweat on his forehead, drenching his hair. He went to the sink. He took the dirty dishes and mugs out of the basin. He let the hot tap run, and squirted some washing-up liquid into the water. He dropped in a cloth. He turned off the tap. He lifted the water – he gave it a go. Down his right side, pain carved a road. He put the basin back in the sink. He leaned against it, got his breath back. That was probably as bad as it was going to get. He hoisted the basin and took it the few steps over to the cooker. The broken mug was still there. It hadn't really smashed. It was broken, but only in two halves, along an old crack. He wrung out the cloth and leaned over the cooker, to get at the coffee stains. But he stopped well short of the wall. The pain pulled him back.

He found the steps beside the back door. The dog was out in the shed. Unless Emer had taken him. If she wasn't in the house. He was tempted to go out there to check. But he didn't. The steps weren't heavy, just awkward. He couldn't lift them properly. They whacked at his shins as he took them over to the cooker. The sweat was in his eyes now. It was cold too; he was freezing. He looked at the wall clock. It was just after three. He unfolded the steps. He waited a while. He wiped the sweat from his eyes and forehead, back into his hair. He grabbed the cloth and got onto the first step. And the next one. The third. He kept his back straight. He could feel the ceiling just over his head. He kneeled on the cooker, on the grille on top of the gas rings. It was a different pain, a normal, stupid pain; he'd take the punishment. He leaned on the wall with his left hand. The road of pain had split in two, the new one curving under the bottom rib across his right side. He'd never be able to get back down. She'd find him like this in the morning. And they'd laugh.

They'd be fine; it wouldn't be too bad. The future measured in box sets. *The Killing* – he'd watch it again, with her. *The Bridge*, *Borgen*. The Danish ones, all the seasons. There was a year in them, at least. He was already picking up a bit of Danish from watching the first season of *Borgen*. *Goddag, kaffe, spin doktor.* He'd get involved in something; he'd volunteer, do what she'd suggested. Something he could care about; there were plenty of things. He'd get a bike, and a backpack. Join a walking club and a choir. He'd read more. He'd have the dinner ready for when she came home from work. He'd follow her out on Fridays, wherever she wanted to go.

He lifted his arm and brought the cloth across some of the stains. They came away nicely. She'd see the clean wall when she got up, or came home. He'd say nothing. He took a breath and lifted his right arm again.

Thirty years of box sets. They were living in a golden age of television drama. He'd read that somewhere. And he believed it.

# The Curfew

He was walking back up the street from the seafront when he looked up and saw the woman coming at him. He'd been watching the leaves. Ex-Hurricane Ophelia was heading towards Dublin and the leaves were blowing the wrong way. They were passing him, dashing by him, rolling up the hill. The curfew would be starting in half an hour. He'd been giving out about it earlier, before his wife left for work. *Do they think there's a civil war? It's only a bit of weather.* But, actually, he liked the drama of it. Even now, walking home – striding, he was striding, a man on a mission – he felt involved, ready, ahead of the coming catastrophe. It was doing him good. He was carrying drugs in a paper bag, but he felt like a man who didn't need them. He'd already folded the garden chairs and put them away, he'd tucked the wheelie bins well in under the hedge. He'd put candles around the house, just in case. He'd done other stuff too. He was all set.

He liked the word – *curfew.* He liked the daft importance of it. There'd be Army tenders patrolling the streets, amplified voices warning citizens to stay in out of the rain. *Get back inside – you'll catch your death!* There'd be bursts of gunfire; blood would flow in the

15

gutters, downhill, while the leaves skipped and swirled up the hill.

He didn't have to visit his mother.

He didn't have to work.

He didn't have to tell his wife about himself and the widow's block.

He'd be safe inside the curfew for a while.

—Bring it on, he said, aloud. There was no one else on the street. Blow, winds, and crack your fuckin' cheeks.

Then he looked up and saw the woman. She was wearing one of those baby slings, and the baby was facing out, looking his way, right under its mother's chin. There were two faces coming straight at him.

It wasn't a baby.

—What should I do? he'd asked.

—Nothing, the doctor had said.

—Nothing?

He'd had a health check a couple of weeks before. A routine check, offered by his health insurer – free. Heart, prostate, eyes, ears. He couldn't remember what else, and all he could really recall was the prostate test. The doctor was a woman, and he hadn't cared. He'd lain on his side and grabbed his knees as she'd told him to, and he'd been fine with it, and pleased, even when he saw her dropping the latex gloves into a bin as she told him he could sit up again. He'd felt modern. It was something he'd never tell his daughters about but would still remember as they lectured him on gender identity or the glass ceiling in Irish universities. I know what you're talking about, he'd be tempted to say. A woman doctor had her finger up my arse, and she was thoroughly professional.

He loved his daughters' lectures.

A week after the check-up, his phone had vibrated in his pocket. He didn't know the number on the screen.

—Hello?

It was the doctor.

—How are you today? she asked.

—Grand, he said. —Yourself?

She told him he had coronary artery disease.

—Oh.

—You shouldn't worry, she said.

—What does it involve? he asked. —Exactly.

She told him there were high levels of cholesterol in his arteries. One of them was 70% blocked.

—70%?

—Yes.

—That's nearly three-quarters, he said.

—We'll need to do further tests, she said. —And again, there's no need to be worrying yourself unduly. It's called the widow's block, by the way.

She sounded cheerful. He liked that.

—The blocked arteries? he asked.

—Yes, she said. —The condition. That's what they call it. The widow's block.

He liked the sound of it. The fact that he had a wife helped. It made sense, somehow. It was almost noble. He was taking the pain for her.

There was no pain. There had been no pain. Not an ache, not a twinge. But now he had a heart problem, a heart condition, a fuckin' disease.

—What should I do?

—Nothing.

—Nothing?

—For now, she said. —You're fine. There'll be further tests, and we'll organise an angiogram. Stents might be wise. But nothing for now. And don't google.

—Okay.

—That way lies madness, she said.

—What's an angiogram? he asked.

—You can google that one, she said. —That's just information.

He liked her. He couldn't remember what she'd looked like.

—Can I google stents?

—You can. But leave it at that.

He put his phone back in his pocket and continued working.

He wrote 'angiogram' on an envelope. He wrote 'stents'. He wrote 'artery' and 'coronary'. And 'nothing'. And 'disease'.

It wasn't a baby in the sling. It was a teddy bear. They – the woman and the bear – had nearly reached him now. He didn't have to move, or shift – sway to the left or right – as he often had to when he encountered people coming the opposite way. They were between trees, him and her, so there was plenty of room on the path.

A teddy bear – a biggish one; it fit neatly into the sling. A baby-sized bear – a big baby. It was wearing a jumper, and it wasn't new. It was older than any baby who might have owned it. He looked at the woman, although he didn't want to; he didn't want to see her looking back at him. He didn't want to be caught. She looked straight ahead. He felt like a spectator watching her through a window. He wasn't there, near her, right beside her.

She passed. He didn't look back. He kept going, up to the house. The curfew was coming, the ex-hurricane was coming. He wanted to check the wheelies again, he wanted to make sure all the windows were fastened. He wanted to get off the street.

She didn't look like a mother.

He didn't know what that meant, really. He could hear himself telling his wife this, and she'd ask him. She was thin, he'd say. She didn't look like a woman who'd recently been pregnant. They'd had four kids of their own; he'd lived in the world of babies and pregnant women. He wasn't a total eejit. She was skinny, he'd say. Very – unusually – skinny. Her face was – the word was there, waiting for him – empty. Her face was empty, he'd say. Vacant. Expressionless. She walked right past me, he'd say, like I wasn't there.

He got his keys out. He'd have the right one ready when he got to the front door.

He remembered the weight of his youngest daughter, Cliona, in one of those slings. They hadn't had one – they might not have been invented yet – for the other kids, the boy and the two older girls. They'd had a backpack thing, like a rucksack, for carrying them.

He'd hated the backpack, six or seven years of having that thing on his back, not being able to see the baby as he walked. He'd hated it until the child was old enough to grab his hair or his collar and he'd know it was fine back there. There was a day in Kerry, on a beach, years ago. The eldest, Ciara, was the baby in the backpack. He'd been up early that morning; it was his turn. He'd put her in the backpack, kissed her forehead, hoisted her onto his back, and gone walking. He hadn't even checked the weather or looked out the window. If you're able to see Brandon in the evening you'll be grand, someone, some oul' lad with a peaked cap had told him. And he'd seen the mountain the night before – he was sure he had. So he'd fed Ciara, shoved a slice of bread into his mouth, and walked out the back door of the house they were renting for the week.

There was a dead whale on the beach, they'd been told when they were eating in the local pub – he couldn't remember the name of the pub or the name of the beach. He'd walked down a lane, crossed the main road, and ten more minutes along a narrow line of tarmac to the beach. Ciara was only eight months, and he hadn't started doing what he did later with the others, talking to them over his shoulder, talking to himself, asking questions they wouldn't be answering. It was early – about seven, he thought; he'd done that thing, taken his watch off when the holidays started – but it was already hot. He reached the sand. The beach was empty, no one else on it at all. The whale, he knew, was to the left. About twenty minutes along the strand, they'd said. *You won't fuckin' miss it, sure.* He'd started walking along the hard sand at the edge of the sea, and somewhere, ten minutes in, he'd decided that Ciara was dead. And he kept walking until he could see the whale, and smell it. He was afraid to stop, submit to the feeling, the certainty he knew was false.

He found it hard to identify that man as himself now, the eejit stepping over the sand. The mad logic of parenthood. He'd stopped when he knew he was smelling the whale. His destination. He couldn't remember the smell; he couldn't remember the words he'd used to describe it when he got back to the house. *Atrocious,* probably; *fuckin' atrocious. Unbelievable – ah, Jesus.* He didn't know. He knew it had been terrible enough to halt him. He could feel it on his skin, adding oil to his sweat. He was about fifty yards from the carcass. He stopped looking at it; he wasn't interested. It was different shades of grey; that was all he remembered. He took off the backpack. He parked it on the sand. Ciara was fine. She was sleeping. He'd remembered to put her sun hat on before he left the house; her neck was properly covered. He'd never told anyone that he thought she was dead, that he'd carried her, dead, for twenty minutes. She was in Vancouver now. She'd be Skyping him later. He hadn't thought of it in years, that day on the beach. He'd never tell her – he didn't know why not.

He was at the front door. But he stepped off the porch and walked back across the small garden to the wheelie bins – brown, green and black. He looked again, made sure they were tucked in under the lip of the hedge, that they wouldn't be lifted by the wind that was coming. He pushed them in further. He didn't know what else to do with them. He could bring them into the house. But he wouldn't. He didn't want his wife to find them lined up in the hall. Maybe he'd look out the bedroom window and see them spinning up, like Dorothy's house in *The Wizard of Oz*. Something to tell Ciara when they were talking. *The brown one landed on the old witch across the street.*

He let himself in.


The house was still empty. The way he'd left it. His wife would be home soon.

She'd have to be. She'd have to get home before the curfew kicked in. Or else she'd be trapped in a spotlight, shot on the front step by some kid in the Army.

He went down, through the house, to the kitchen.

He took the tablets, the three slim boxes, out of the chemist's paper bag. His new pills. His regimen. He

21

put them standing in a row. They looked unfinished like that. He needed more boxes. Stonehenge. He could make a joke of it when he was telling her later.

He got his reading glasses from the table. He'd left them on top of the book he was reading; he always did that. *The Road to Unfreedom: Russia, Europe, America.* They could all fuck off till he'd taken his pills, and found out what it was that he was taking.

He'd loved carrying the youngest girl, Cliona. Any excuse, almost literally any excuse, he'd slide her into the sling, her face looking out at the world, and go off – to the shops, town, the seafront, nowhere. He'd loved the weight there against his chest and the fact that he saw what she was seeing. He could feel her excitement, her legs hopping, the approaching faces breaking into smiles for her, then for him. *She's gorgeous. She's a dote.* Proud of his daughter, proud of himself. Cliona in the sling, Conor in the buggy, Ciara and Maeve on either side holding the handle. Down through town, through the crowds, Henry Street, Grafton Street. People made way, he never lost a child.

The doctor had sent him leaflets in the post. *The Fats of Life – The Lowdown on High Cholesterol* was one of them. He wasn't fat. He hadn't read it yet; he'd glanced at it. There was an article about some smiling actor from *Fair City* who'd 'taken control of his cholesterol' and a page called 'Recipe Corner'. There was another leaflet. *Angioplasty & Coronary Stenting.* There were no pictures in that one. Definitions, questions answered, a detachable consent form at the back. He hadn't read that one, either.

He took his glasses off the book and went back to Stonehenge. He listened, for whistling wind, falling branches, roof slates decapitating pensioners.

He remembered Hurricane Charley – in 1986, he thought it was. He'd sat on his bed all night and waited for the windows to fly in on top of him, shred the curtains, impale him against the wall. He'd lived alone then. It was the last time he'd felt physically frightened; he thought that was true. And that was more than thirty years ago.

He looked at the three boxes.

—The maximum dose, she'd said, the cardiologist, this morning when he met her. —To be on the safe side.

—Okay.

—One piece of advice.

—Yes?

—Don't google, she'd said.

—Your colleague said that as well.

—Good, she'd said. —You know enough for now. You'll pick up more as we go along.

She was looking at him over her glasses, as if she'd stopped being just a doctor and had become his new friend. He wondered later, when he was looking at the scrambled eggs he'd ordered in the café across from the hospital, and the little portion of silver-foiled butter for the toast, if that was him, seeing her like that, or if it was her, part of her training or her personality. He'd taken the advice; he hadn't googled 'coronary artery disease'.

He looked at the boxes. He picked up the biggest one. *Rosuvastatin Teva Pharma*. It sounded like a star or a planet. 40 milligrams. The maximum dose, the cardiologist had said. That fact had impressed him.

—We need to get the cholesterol right down to where it should be.

—Okay.

*May cause dizziness*, a label on the box said. He picked up one of the other boxes. The same thing – *May cause*

*dizziness. If affected, do not drive or operate machinery.*
Did that include his laptop? Or the printer. He'd joke
about that too when he was telling his wife. *I fell off the
laptop. Within seconds of taking the things.*

There was a leaflet – another leaflet; death by fuckin'
leaflet – inside the box. He unfolded it. It looked a bit
like the instructions that came with a washing machine
or a blender. *Read all this leaflet carefully before you start
taking this medicine because it contains important information for you.* He'd never read a leaflet in his life. He
thought that was literally true.

—Decide on a time of day, the cardiologist had told
him. —Morning, evening – whatever suits.

He didn't want to become the man who forgot his
pills, or the man who remembered his fuckin' pills. He
could hear his father. *Where are my pills, where did I
leave my pills?* – the refrain that had made the grandkids, his kids, laugh whenever they heard it. They still
said it, ten years after his father's funeral, when they
were looking for the salt on the table or a missing sock
under a bed – when they were home.

He had no grandkids to entertain with his pills. He'd
take them – the pills – in the morning, with the porridge. He'd told the cardiologist that he ate porridge
every morning. *Oh, that's great, that's helpful.* Three
tablets – he'd call them tablets; it was better, more
adult, than pills. *Where are my tablets, where did I leave
my tablets?* One of each, once a day. Two statins, one
aspirin. It wasn't complicated. He'd manage. He'd
opened the two other boxes. One of the pill cards had
the days of the week on serrated squares – *Mon. Tue.
Wed.* Did that mean he'd have to wait till Monday
before he started? If he started now, he'd be taking his
Monday pill – his Monday tablet – on a Wednesday.

He was fuckin' wild. He stood and got himself a glass of water. He had a look out the kitchen window while he was at it. The branches on the tree next door were waving; they were bending. He could hear a siren, off somewhere. He could hear wires whistling – he thought he could.

—Where are my pills?

His mother came running. Running in her slippers, in from the kitchen.

—Where are your pills?

—That's what I'm bloody asking. Where are they?

She was afraid her husband would fall dead if they didn't find the pills. He'd nearly died; she'd witnessed what could happen. He'd had a heart attack, and a triple bypass. He was sitting opposite her at the kitchen table, then his face was in his soup and she could see the sweat running off the top of his head. *Like a tap, it was – like a waterfall.* She'd phoned him, her son, and told him about the ambulance arriving, the men with the stretcher coming into the house. He'd gone over and driven her to Beaumont – the hospital. He'd looked at her face, the side of her face – the fear, the tension. She didn't look like his mother.

—What was the soup? he'd asked her.

—Cream of vegetable, she'd said.

And she'd smiled.

—Terrible waste.

Finding the pills, knowing exactly where they were – that was the important thing. She'd spent years looking for his pills, keeping his father alive. Until the grandkids started to make a joke of it, and the fuckin' old tyrant decided to join in.

But he'd seen it before it became part of the fun of every Sunday afternoon. He'd seen his mother's face and his father's, her terror and his glee, before the kids turned it into a weekly bit of crack.

—Where are my pills?

He wouldn't have pills; they'd be tablets. He'd know where they were. He wouldn't become his father.

He put them on top of the fridge. He typed a note into his phone: *tablets = fridge*.


He sat on the bed. He could see the trees on the street, and the leaves falling, the chestnut leaves – huge brown hands – dropping, floating, caught by the wind and rolling uphill. If he lifted himself slightly, he'd see the wheelies tucked under the hedge. A guy on a bike went past. His hood was fat, full of the hurricane. That was all the drama – the guy on the bike.

It was half-past two. He'd listened to the lunchtime news. The west of the country was being chewed by the weather; there were power cuts, roads made impassable, tin roofs pulled off farm sheds. Outside – here, in Dublin – it was a windy day. That was all. He'd been sitting on the bed, waiting. He wanted to see a car in the air, a hundred-year-old oak toppling; he wanted to witness something – anything.

And he didn't.

The leaves were the story. The fact that nothing was happening. The leaves going the wrong way, and the woman with the teddy bear. They were his stories.

He lay back on the bed. He turned, into whiteness and nothing – no thoughts or things. He slept.

★

He woke with an ache in his right arm; the ache – the pain – had woken him. Was that a sign? Was it pain in the right or the left arm that was a prelude to a heart attack? Or was that the shoulder? He didn't know; he wouldn't look it up. His arm was numb – just numb, the way he'd been lying on it. His wife had told him he slept with his arms folded, as if he'd been sitting in a chair and had fallen off it, straight onto the bed. He hadn't believed her.

—Not every night, he'd protested.

—Yes – every night.

—How do you know?

—I see you.

—You're awake?

—Sometimes.

—Why?

—Jesus, there's a question.

She was there now. She was sitting where he'd been sitting before he fell asleep. He felt her weight on the mattress first, and saw her back. She was looking out the window. It was dark.

—Anything happening out there?

—Not really, she said. —Ex-hurricanes aren't what they used to be.

—Like everything else.

He'd have to tell her. He had the widow's block and she was going to be the widow.

—You made it home before the curfew, he said.

—Just about, she said.

He hadn't moved. He didn't want to sit up. He liked looking at her, from where he was, where she was. He'd always liked looking at her.

—Have we food? she asked.

—Loads.

—Grand.

—I put candles all around the house. Just in case.

—We can pretend it's a spa.

She hadn't moved. She hadn't turned to look at him. He leaned over a bit – the numbness in his arm had gone – and put his hand on her back. He felt her move, and her hand touched his, just brushed across it.

—Get up, she said. —And we'll watch the news. All the action is over in the west. In Galway and Kerry and the other lovely places.

—The wild Atlantic way.

—There you go.

He sat up now.

—I saw a thing, he said.

He told her about the woman he'd seen, the woman with the teddy bear.

—That's so sad, she said.

He heard her shoes fall onto the floor, and now she was sitting beside him.

He'd tell her in a minute. He'd tell her about his tablets and his heart.

—I miss the kids, he said.

He started to cry.

# Life Without Children

Once, years ago, when the children were children, someone had asked Alan if he had any – children. And he'd
said No.

He hadn't expected to say it; it hadn't been part of
a plan. It wasn't a woman he was talking to. It wasn't
the possibility of sex that had pushed him to say it. He
remembered it as a choice, a junction, Yes or No. And –
just the once – he'd gone for No and for the rest of
the evening he'd been a man with no children.

It had been dreadful, really, having to constantly
remind himself that he had no kids. Because that was
what he had been, for more than two decades – the man
with kids. From the second he woke to that point in the
night when he stopped knowing his eyes were closing,
he'd been that man. And the evening he'd denied it he'd
still been that man, out for the night with no witnesses
but still up past his neck in four childhoods.

It felt like the worst thing he'd ever done. For years.
He'd been Peter in the Garden of wherever, denying
four little Jesuses. He knew that if it had been a woman
and the denial had led to sex, he'd have shouted something as he was coming – in a room off a room, in the
back of her car. He'd have groaned it: *I've four kids*.

He'd have yelped their names in order of age, from the youngest up. *Then Lizzie – she'll be doing her Junior Cert next year!*

But there hadn't been sex.

And now, he actually was the man with no children. They weren't in the house. They weren't in his head when he woke. Their names on the screen when his phone rang were often a shock; nothing in the house or in the rhythm of his day was a reminder. They were gone.

He wasn't a father.

What was he? A sixty-two-year-old bachelor. With a wife. And she was a sixty-year-old spinster, with an occasional husband. They'd become brother and sister, somehow.

That was shite – just nonsense. He was feeling hard done by, sorry for himself. But he wasn't – not now. He had felt that way for a long time. When he realised that he wasn't needed any more, needed in the way that had defined him, to himself, for so long. When his youngest girl had shouted at him to shut the bathroom door. When he'd stood outside on the landing and felt like an intruder, a boor, a dangerous man. He'd fallen into something that he thought now might have been depression – he didn't know. He'd waited outside, afraid to move, terrified he'd lost his child because he'd opened the door while she, his youngest, his baby, Lizzie, sat on the toilet. He wanted to be there when she came out. He wanted to be ready with something apologetic and funny. But he saw it, the big, dejected, wet-eyed man blocking the exit, filling the landing with himself. He went down the stairs and – he knew this – he was a different man when he got to the bottom.

But that night – back to that night when he'd said he had no children. He'd done nothing with it. He'd

30

gone home. He'd checked on the kids. He'd gone to bed and slept. He'd been up before everyone in the morning.

But it had been a moment, that night – a different life out in front of him, if he'd wanted it.

And now: it's another one. Another moment.


He's in England – he's in Newcastle. He's just off the phone to his wife, in Dublin. The pubs have been closed at home and the cinemas and theatres. The schools have been shut for a week. Social distancing is a phrase that everyone understands. It's like gender fluidity and sustainable development. They're using the words like they've been translated from Irish, in the air since before the English invaded.

But he's in England, and it hasn't happened yet. There are no yellow-and-black warning signs. The pubs are roaring, the streets are packed.

—When are you home, Al? Sinéad had asked him.
—Remind me.
—Sunday, he'd said.

He didn't tell her that the bar downstairs is wide open and mad in the early Friday afternoon, full past the walls with a stag party, about thirty drunk men in *Hawaii Five-O* shirts. Knocking back double and treble shots in pint glasses. Sweating, coughing, wheezing men, barking, and whacking one another. They're from Belfast, he thinks. It's going to end in tears. It's going to end in blood.

The taxi driver from the train station had put it all in its place.

—The Coroona carry-on, he said. —It's a lood a shite.

Alan had laughed but he'd opened the passenger window, to let some air in. In the hotel foyer he didn't want to put his hands on the counter. He didn't want to hand over his debit card. He wasn't going to get into the lift. It had just opened behind him. Six or seven of the Belfast/Hawaii lads poured out, clutching phones and pint glasses. He'd carried his case up the stairs.

He wants to go home; he needs to get home. But there's something in him, too: he's loving it.

It's a moment. He knows. He can stay here. He can disappear. Into England. Be the man with no children. No country. The man with nothing at all.

He washes his hands for – he'd be guessing – fifteen seconds. He wipes the door handles with a towel. He wipes the handle of his case. He opens the case and takes out what he'll need – a shirt, socks. He wipes the handle again. He throws the towel in the bath. He takes it out and hangs it on the door. He sits on the bed. He looks at the remote control on the table beside the bed. He doesn't touch it.

He's become an anxious man. Not today – not just today, after talking to Sinéad and scrolling through the news from Ireland. He's been constantly checking his watch, checking the calendar, checking the day, checking everything – for years now. He'd look at Sinéad's expression. Was she happy – was she happy with him? He wondered if he was talking to himself, after he become aware that he was hissing as he walked uphill, and counting the gates to his own gate. Was he doing it out loud? He'd put a shirt beside a pair of jeans on top of the bed at home and wondered if they clashed, if he could wear them together – to the shops, to the pub, downstairs to the kitchen. He didn't remember caring when he was younger. His parents had died; he was the oldest person he knew well. This pleased him and kept him awake. He'd left the back door open; he'd forgotten to leave out the black wheelie; he'd forgotten the name of the animal that built the dams. In the nature programme he'd been half-watching before he came up to bed.

This is his chance. He's ready to go.

He's forgotten the name of that animal again.

This is the chance, to sweat out the fear, to join a new life. He'll go down to the lads in the hotel bar. He doesn't have a *Hawaii 5-O* shirt; nothing in his case will remind anyone of *Hawaii 5-O*. There's a pink shirt. He won't smell it first. He'll just hold it by the shoulders and give it a snap, scare some of the creases out of it. He'll order three gins in a tumbler and slip in among the lads. He'll talk if he needs to; he'll put on the accent that irritates Sinéad when they're watching the News. *There's a wee riot.* He'll work out if they're Catholics or Prods. He's on his way, already his new self.

Beaver.

That's the buck-toothed fucker that builds the dams.

He'll need a name when he goes down there. His own name is probably neutral but he doesn't want it. Mick, Mike, Pete, Stu, Jim, Dave, Shamie, wee Beaver – he hasn't a clue; they all feel like landmines. He'll bypass the lads and head straight out into Newcastle.

He takes off the pink shirt and puts on the last clean one. He takes his passport out of his wallet. He'll put it in the case, in the bag with the dirty laundry. He should bring it with him, fling it into the Tyne, slip it into a bin. If he's being serious, that's what he should do.

He's out of the room. He stops the door with his foot. He checks that the room key is in his wallet. It is – he's on his way.

He's smiling. He's made himself smile. This is him not being himself.

The lift doors slide open. The lift is empty. He steps in. The heat, the smell of aftershave, thrown on by men who haven't shaved. He holds his breath, he leans on nothing, presses the button with his elbow. It's only two floors. He'd forgotten not to get into the lift. He'll use the stairs from now on.

From now on? He won't be staying here. He might not come back. There's a couple of shirts, a jumper, his passport, the case. That's all that's up there. And his iPad – it's on the bed. He can feel the warmth of the men on his skin, he can see their breath – the droplets – in the air in front of him. He feels the lift stop, the little jolt. He's out, sideways, before the doors are fully open. He can inhale now, if he's careful. He hears the lads in the bar; he hears glass hitting the floor tiles.

More sliding doors – he's out. He can breathe. This air came over the North Sea; it's too cold for any virus. He's on a hill above the river. As far as he understands, he's not actually in Newcastle; he's in Gateshead. Newcastle is the other side of the river. He can see his route there. Across a road, around a building site, over a wide car park, to steps that he's sure will bring him down to the river and the pedestrian bridge he can see shining below him. He can see plenty of people on the Newcastle side but it's quiet here. There's no traffic at all on the road; there's no one working on the building site. The car park gives him the creeps. Old potholed tarmac; there are only four or five cars parked in space for hundreds. One of the cars starts just as he's walking past it. He doesn't look through the windscreen. He doesn't look back, the tyres don't crunch over the tarmac. He's at the steps, down to the river.

He checks his phone. There's a message – from Sinéad. He won't stop here. He'll wait till he gets some-where, a pub or something, where he can read it properly and answer – if he answers.

Of course he'll answer.

He mightn't.

He's crossing the river. This is the bit where he should be lobbing his passport into the water. And his phone. Into the river without breaking stride. Whistling 'Fog on the Tyne'. The river will still be there when he's coming back – if he's coming back. His boarding pass for the flight home is on his phone. Everything is on the phone. The bank, the passwords, the photos, the life. He'll have a few pints and a pizza, then decide.

He's crossing the bridge and already planning on crossing back over the bridge, returning before he arrives. He's slowing down; he can feel it in his legs. The doubts and the dread – they're turning him back. It's familiar. It's been going on for a long time. He's been carrying the virus for years.

Drivel.

Sentimental, self-pitying drivel.

He stops halfway across, but not to turn back. It's the other bridges. The five, maybe six metal bridges that span the river. They're great – they're beautiful. From where he stands, if he shifts slightly, they seem like one elaborate bridge. He gets out the phone, takes a photo. He deletes it and puts the phone back into his pocket. He doesn't want the photo or the urge to send it. He's moving again. The energy's back in his legs. He's in Newcastle now – officially.

He climbs up a street from the river. There's a gang of women coming at him. They're all big, all in black skirts and T-shirts, with pink sashes across their chests, and big pink bunny ears. There are seven or eight of them; they're singing a song he doesn't know. It's a hen group, although it's hard to pick out the hen. One of them shouts just as they reach him.

—Tracey wants some cock!

She's not looking at him as she shouts. It's not a threat or an invitation.

She does it again.

—Tracey wants some cock!

—She fooking does too!

They're around him, almost going over him. He can feel their heat, the mass of them; he can see the eyeshadow sliding down from the eyes, the shining cheeks. It's early evening. The droplets they'll inhale tonight, they'll be dead in days. *Here lies Tracey. She wanted some cock.*

Sinéad has told him that social distancing has become almost natural at home. She's told him about the polite slalom that walking down the SuperValu aisles has become in the week that he's been gone. Not here, he'll tell her – he wants to tell her. There's no distance between the bodies here.

There's another gang of women – they're not girls, they're way too old for girls – charging down the hill. It's all hills, this town. They're in pink this time, with black sashes and no ears. A more sedate group. They're not shouting for cock.

There's a pub across the way that looks promising, one of the BrewDog places he's read about. He'll wait till the pink hens pass, before he crosses. He should be following them, he thinks. This is supposed to be his new life.

He'll need cash. He'll have to go to an ATM. He'll have to tap the silver buttons with a finger. He'll have to push his card into a slot that infected stags and hens have been rubbing and coughing on all day. He'll have to do it – touch things, breathe sweat. He really should follow those women. The pink or the black gang. He should follow them into whatever bar they commandeer and dive right in. They'll pour their drinks over him. They'll sit on him. They'll kill him.

He stood in another hotel room a few days before – he thinks it was in Manchester – and looked at himself in the mirror as he came out of the bathroom. He saw his father's legs. Just for a second, they weren't his, Alan's. He was sitting on sand beside his brother – they were in Cahore, in Wexford – and he was looking at their father as he walked up from the sea, and he came closer and closer and he stopped in front of them and Alan looked through his father's legs as a black dog and three children ran beside the water, from his father's left ankle to his other one. His father's legs were the door to the sea. They were pale – it must have been early in the summer – and they were hairless, unlike his arms and his chest – and there was a line like a river, a blue vein, running down one shin. He stood in front of the hotel room mirror and saw that vein in his own leg. He almost looked behind him, to watch his father coming out of the bathroom. His father had been dead for seven years. They were his own legs but he'd become his father. *You're a ringer for your dad.* People had said it at the funeral. *It's fuckin' uncanny.* He had the legs of a dead man. *I'll say this,* an old friend of his father's had said that day, beside the hearse. He held on to Alan's hand, and wouldn't give it back. *You're not half the man your father was. I'll leave it at that.*

★

He looks in the pub window. The place is nearly empty. It makes no sense. Both sides of the street are heaving but there are only two punters inside. They're together, a woman and a man – close to his age, he thinks – but they're not talking. He looks away, and back to the window, in case it's a trick of the light, the late after-noon sun hiding a line of people sitting at the bar. But no – there's no change; it's still just the two in there.

It's his kind of place, a quiet pub in a mad town. A few weeks ago, even yesterday, he'd have been straight in – straight in on his father's legs. He'd have been looking through the menu for an IPA with a daft name he could photograph and send to his family and a couple of friends. To remind them – and himself – that he wasn't where he normally was. He'd have opened Google Maps and checked the route from the bar stool back to the hotel. He'd have ordered his pint – Born to Die, or Clockwork Tangerine – and he'd have quickly persuaded himself that it made good sense to eat there too – a burger or a pizza – and he'd have been back in the hotel before dark.

The pull of the empty pub is strong. But he resists and moves on up the hill, on his own legs.

He'd have emailed the kids. He'd have made sure they all got their own message. He'd have written the one, then adjusted it for each – a verb, a noun, a musical reference. He'd have spent half the night cutting and pasting. One pint was the limit for that kind of work.

But he's the man with no kids.

He could turn back. Not to the hotel, to the BrewDog pub. A slow pint of Punk IPA – what a name; fuckin' mad; hilarious – and a photo home, the family Whats-App: *Are the pubs shut over there? xx.*

Here's his chance, though. He'll find a Wetherspoon's, walk right into the happy hour and death. He's sweating. The hill is a killer, never mind the virus. He doesn't want to get used to the words and terms, their meanings and consequences – Covid, cluster, at-risk, asymptomatic. He doesn't want the carefulness. This way is freedom, back home is boredom and terror. He can walk up this hill to the life he never had, or walk back down to the life he doesn't want. He's still feeling exhilarated, although he has to check first. He believes what he's doing – he does. He's still out in the air, though. He's socially distant. He hasn't burrowed into the crowd. He's a bit mad, and tired. And a bit feverish, maybe. His throat is dry. But that's from the climb. He's anxious.

This is what he has to stop. The roll call of the adjectives. The running commentary that comes with everything he does and thinks. The self-assessments that have always crippled him. *You're shit, you're weak, you're just not good enough.*

Is he anxious now, though? He isn't. *He thinks he isn't anxious. But he isn't sure.* He doesn't know what time it is. He doesn't know the name of the street. He could turn back and go straight down to the river and he'd see the hotel on the other side. But that's not the point. He'll turn a corner soon, and another – more than likely. And he won't note them, or care. He's bringing his sense of direction – it's good, it's reliable. But he won't be using it.

There's a rubbish bin up ahead.

He takes out his phone.

The bin's overflowing. There are wasps bopping around it. At this time of year? At this time of day? He pushes the phone down, under a squashed McDonald's bag, and further down. He lets go of it. He makes himself walk away. It's the hardest thing he's ever done.

But he's done it. He's done the mad thing.

They were at a party, about a year before. But he couldn't tell any more if it was a party or just a group of people standing around in the same house.

He'd said it to Sinéad on the way home in the taxi.

—Was that a party, was it?

—What?

—Were we at a party there?

He could see the driver's eyes in the rear-view, looking away.

—What d'you mean? she asked.

—Well, he said. —Parties. They used to be obvious.

They'd met at a party. He'd caught her as she started to fall backwards down the stairs with a bottle of Heineken in each hand.

—But tonight, he said. —For fuck sake. Is it our age?

—No one vomited, she said. —Is that what you mean? Is that what you're pining for?

—Kind of, he said. —It was just a bit of a non-event. Wasn't it?

—I enjoyed it, she said.

—Did you?

—Not really, she said. —No.

—No, he'd said. —Me too.

—We missed *Succession*, Al.

He'd laughed.

The man of the house had wanted to show Alan his desk. Alan hardly knew him; they met maybe twice a year. He knew him because he was married to Orla, who had gone to school with Sinéad's sister. He didn't have his number or email, and he had to remind himself of the man's name – Geoff – every time they were about to meet. It had occurred to Alan tonight that Geoff had done the same thing, half an hour before they'd arrived. He'd asked Orla what Sinéad's husband was called. He remembered women's names; it was the men who were vague. But Geoff worked at home – Alan hadn't a clue what he did – and he'd got himself a desk that allowed him to stand as he worked.

—That must be some fuckin' desk, said another of the husbands. —If you have to ask its permission if you want to stand up.

—I have a back thing, Geoff told them, and some of the other men had nodded. They had back things too.

Alan had gone upstairs to the toilet and Geoff had followed him up.

—I'll show it to you when you get out, he said, as Alan shut the jacks door.

—Grand.

He'd spent a good while washing his hands and there was no sign of Geoff when he came out. There was no one on the landing. But he heard the voice.

—Alan?

—Yeah?

—I'm in here.

There was an open door to Alan's right. He went to the door and looked in. There was a long desk – it looked like a delicatessen counter – almost across the width of the room. There was a laptop, closed, and a lamp. There was Geoff. There was a mattress in one of the corners.

—I sleep there, said Geoff.

He looked at Alan.

Alan said nothing. He looked at the desk. He looked at Geoff. The man knew no one. He'd no one else he could tell. Alan remembered the walls. They were pink. It had been a daughter's bedroom.

He didn't tell Sinéad. He couldn't. He wouldn't have got past the walls. He'd have cried.

—Will we watch it when we get home?

—It's too late.

—Go on, Al, she said. —Be wild.

—Okay, he said. —A bit of it. I might fall asleep.

—That's permitted.


He's got rid of the phone.

He's happy with that. It seems enough – the act, the protest. He turns and heads back down the street. He'll have the pint in the BrewDog pub. He'll order a pizza, a spicy one that will make his head sweat. He'll go back to the hotel. He'll go up the stairs, to his room. He'll wash his hands for twenty seconds. He'll take his shoes off and get up on the bed. He'll use his iPad to change his flight to tomorrow morning. He'll call Sinéad on his iPad. He'll tell her he lost his phone. He'll tell her his new flight details. He'll tell her what he's seen and heard tonight. He'll tell her that Tracey wants some cock.

# Gone

She left the day before the lockdown. Her keys were on the table in the kitchen. When I saw them I just thought, She's after forgetting her keys again, I'll have to stay here till she gets home. But then I thought, You're not going anywhere – be a bit reasonable. And if she'd been there, I'd have apologised – if that makes sense. I thought of the other times she'd gone out of the house without her keys. I could only think of two. And I felt quite good about that – because that was one of the things we'd been talking about. Me always thinking the worst. But I didn't think the worst this time. I stopped myself. I was self-aware. In the kitchen. So. I looked at the keys again. The way they were positioned on the table. In the middle. The centre. Between the salt and the pepper. Like Exhibit A. A message. I don't know what I felt then. I mean, I'd only been to Lidl. Just getting a few things. And I'd brought a bag of old books to the Vincent de Paul shop. Mostly her books, by the way. Not that that matters. But I'd only been gone maybe an hour. Tops. But the keys – there, like that. I phoned her. And it started to ring. Her phone started ringing. In the cutlery drawer. It was like I was watching – I was *in* – a crime thing. The phone rings, I look across at the cutlery drawer, then there's the ad for Volvo or Casillero del Diablo. But it was only for a second. I was in the kitchen, alone – no sign of a camera crew – and her phone was in the cutlery drawer. It stopped ringing.

About the phone – I haven't a clue. I didn't bring it. That's all.

It was a distraction – that was what it was. Because once I found it, I stopped worrying. It wasn't the dramatic beat before the ads. Not in this story. I was in a different story. And it wasn't crime; it was comedy. Because of the cutlery drawer. And the thing about the cutlery drawer – it was an issue. It was a running joke that wasn't very funny. That I thought was a bit cruel. Before she moved in, I never even used the word cutlery. Knives, forks. Spoons, if they were there – I'll stir my tea with the butt of a knife. I don't care if I slide open the drawer and find the knives mixed in with the spoons or the corkscrew hiding under the forks. I'm not fussy. Or obsessed – the way she said I was. But I do think it's reasonable to be able to find a spoon within, say, five seconds of opening the drawer. And I think it's okay to be angry when I go to open the drawer but I can't do it properly because the sliding mechanism, the runner, is bent – it's actually buckled – because someone else attempted to shove a ball of twine into the drawer and kept on shoving even though the ball was much too big. That was what happened – she broke the bloody drawer and it suddenly became about me. Because I took everything out. The cheque book stubs, the three potato peelers, the fuckin' twine, the chopsticks – hundreds of them, no exaggeration – the deck of cards, the snow globe – from the Canaries! – the paperclips, the bills, receipts, menus, the egg beater, the stale cornflakes. I laid it all out on the counter, and I was trying to straighten, to fix, the runner – and I succeeded – when she came in. And she was horrible about it. Defensive, I suppose. The buckled runner was my problem. Because I'd made it a problem. From then on, she couldn't walk into the kitchen without saying something about the cutlery drawer. She'd go over and open it, really pull at the handle. A plane went down in the Pacific, she'd say – something like that, some item from the news. Is it in here? She'd leave it open. I laughed at first. But it went on too long. I'd open it and find a pair of knickers or a flip-flop. Or – once – the remote control. And that takes effort. You decide to bring this thing through the house and put it into the cutlery drawer. Anyway, she'd done the same trick before – put *my* phone in the cutlery drawer and phoned me. Twice. I'm sick of those words – cutlery drawer.

It was a decision. Just, I hadn't packed a bag in my head or thought about what I'd need to take from the bathroom. Made lists. Or what I'd do for money – how we'd manage that. But when I heard the word. Lockdown. I was out of the house. Out of that life. I shut the door after me. And I decided to go back in and leave the keys. It was all deliberate. I was thinking – deciding what I was doing, as I went. And I was gone again, on my way – where, though? – when I realised that I didn't have my phone. I didn't know I hadn't taken it. And I couldn't get back in, because the keys

45

were inside. So I decided I was doing it the old-fashioned way. I was disappearing. My grandfather played football with a man who disappeared. He was watching a programme, a documentary – years ago this was, when I was little. My grandfather was half-watching, and there was one of those team photographs, from way back, the 1940s it must have been, and he saw himself in the back row. It was his team – I can't remember what they were called. The man who'd disappeared was in the front row, and my grandfather knew him. He'd forgotten all about the story. I think he'd married my granny and moved away when it happened – when the man walked out of his own house and didn't come back. But apparently, he'd been in England all that time, for decades, and one of his daughters – she had children of her own by this stage – she opened her door after someone rang the bell, and there he was. Her father. But that was possible back then. Disappearing. No internet footprints or bank cards, or – I don't know – findmydad.ie. That's why I left my phone behind, I think. And everything on it. Those details – the passwords – all you need. I didn't want them. I was at the bus stop – I hadn't even thought about taking the car, although it's mine. But I saw the bus coming and I went to get the phone from my pocket – my jacket pocket. It was in one of those foldable holders, like a wallet. My Leap card and debit card and one or two other things were in it. And that was when I knew that I didn't have the phone, and I let the bus go past. I'd no phone, no money – nothing. I was doing exactly what I wanted to do.

*

46

I put the phone beside her keys, on the table. For when she got home – she'd see them there. And then, I think I got the things I'd bought and put them away. There wasn't that much. I didn't go to Lidl thinking it was the end of the world. I knew the lockdown – what we now call the lockdown – was coming. But I don't think I knew – I don't think I understood – how extensive, how literal, it was going to be. The schools were shut but I don't have children. Now. There was a film I wanted to see, *Dark Waters* – with Mark Ruffalo in it. I was half-thinking I'd go in to Cineworld that night, before the cinemas closed. I wasn't panicking, I suppose is what I'm trying to get across. About food and toilet paper, or Laura. I knew I'd more than likely be working from home but I had that all sorted, ready to go. If it happened, it happened. I think that was probably my attitude. My philosophy. I remember shouting her name. To check that she wasn't in the house – or was. I stayed at the bottom of the stairs for a while. I think I called her name again. Then I think I put the green wheelie out onto the street. I remember negotiating the space between the car and the wall, getting it out through the gap. The fact that the car was there told me – suggested – that she hadn't gone far. Although neither of us used it much. The last time we'd been in the car together was that time in early February, when we went to see her sister in Kilkenny. Her sister has this big place, a farmhouse that Protestants lived in once, I'd say. Five kids and ponies and a pig. And a husband who worked in one of the outhouses and hardly came out. I think we saw him once while we were there. Which was fine, because he's a prick. Laura would agree with me, and her sister definitely would. We made love that night. She insisted on it, although I didn't take

47

much persuading. She wanted us to fuck in her sister's house. She said that in the car on the way down. I asked if we could get a quick rehearsal in, if I found somewhere to park – I was driving. She laughed. And if I was to stop there – if I was to look at her then, remember her like that, laughing at what I'd said – I'd be completely lost as to what happened. After. Only a month – a bit more. Five weeks – six. She seemed happy. I know I was. At that moment.

I didn't want Jim, or anyone else, to be able to point and say, She went that way. I didn't want to follow a route or leave any pointers behind me. But I had to go somewhere, so I went to a friend's house. She lives by herself, nearby. I don't know her that well, actually. But I like her and I remembered exactly where her house was; I'd been to a party there once. So that's where I went. I'm not going to talk about what happened then. Just: I stayed there for a day and I got into a place of my own – not literally my own, but somewhere I could stay for a while – on the first full day of the lockdown. I moved when nobody else did. It was perfect. I walked down the middle of the street. No one saw me.

I looked at the phone. I remember this. I'd made a kind of a bolognese sauce and I'd left spaghetti beside the pot, uncooked, for when she got in, if she wanted it. I put my fork down and I picked up the phone. I knew the password – her mother's birthday. I'd used it before, when she'd asked me to. But I'd never done this. I'd never opened her phone without her knowing about it. But I did now. I didn't like doing it, but I thought it was okay. I'd look at her texts and emails. I'd only read the recent ones, any she got or had sent earlier, or the day before. I'll admit, I was nervous. What if there was something, a story I knew nothing about? A man – or even a woman. Or something else – anything. And I do wonder – I still do. Why was I nervous – suddenly? Only when I picked up the phone. Only then, at that second, a bit like an electric shock running up my arm, across my shoulder, through my jaw: I realised she had a life when I wasn't looking. And I knew she'd gone. I put her phone back down. I didn't look at her texts or emails. I didn't look for clues.

Two people knew what I'd done. Two women – friends. They made phone calls and I was in an Airbnb place, rent-free, for as long as the lockdown lasted. Then they left me alone. Because I asked them to. I knew I had no job to go to; the boss had warned us. I could claim the Covid dole. I had a current account I hadn't used in a long time, and I started to use that. I got it sorted and stayed away from email after that. I was amazed at how empty the world was, how compliant the city became. Because I wasn't – compliant. I wandered. After dark. On my new legs. Wearing someone else's clothes. I gave myself a new history. I'd no siblings; I was an only child. Although that wasn't strictly true. I'd had a brother but he died when I was very young; he was older than me. He died in a freak accident, kicked by a cow. I made up my new self as I wandered. I kept turning left, say, no matter how narrow or unpromising the turn. Down lanes packed with feral cats and dumped rubbish bags. Another night, I'd skip the first two turns, then take the next right and keep turning right. I always found my way back. My father shot himself, out in the barn, two years after my brother died. He blamed himself for what had happened. My mother was alive but had dementia; she didn't know me. She was in a care home, in Kildare. I hadn't heard her say my name in ten years. I'd never been much of a walker before. I've never had boots or a waxed jacket or sticks or any of the gear I've seen in other people's cars. But I walked now, when no one else did. I gave myself names. I'd set off as Nelly and I'd see how it felt as I went. I tried Nina too, and Sadie. But I gave up. I didn't need a new name. And I didn't need the biography either. I have a sister. (I'd called her, using my friend's phone, and told her I was fine but I'd be away, off the grid, for a while. She sighed, as if she'd been expecting me to say this. I asked her to tell Mammy and I asked her not to contact Jim, and to tell Mammy not to. She sighed again and told me I was being selfish. I agreed with her. Probably, I said. You'll be killing Mammy. I'm sorry, I said, and hung up.) My father didn't put a gun barrel into his mouth in a barn. He isn't a farmer. My mother cuts the crossword out of the *Sunday Times* and puts it beside the kettle, with a blue biro, and has it finished by the following Sunday, always. She collects the finished ones, ties them with a rubber band, and keeps them in a biscuit tin. You're to show that lot to the HSE, she says, if they ever come looking for me. She likes me, that version of my mother – she approves of me. She came to me – that line, and the twinkle in her eye – when I was reading the signs in the windows of a row of shops I'd never walked past before. There was a chemist, a bakery, a Spar. They were all the same, with the yellow-and-black warning signs. But there was one piece of white paper, a bookie's docket, just two words hand-printed, taped to the window of Paddy Power. Fuck This, it said. To think of someone doing that, waiting for the opportunity, just before the shop was shut for the lockdown. Knowing that it might never be noticed – it was in the bottom corner, near the door. It made me happy, and I decided it was me; I'd done it. And I decided that my mother kept her crosswords as proof that her mind still did what she told it to. I didn't lick it off a stone. We could look at each other and grin. I was a cardboard model and I kept putting on and taking off dresses and skirts and bras and boots, stilettos and hair, and parents and siblings, and names and partners and husbands and lovers and exes. There was no one out there to stop me. I could do what I wanted. No one looked.

I'd shout her name. Before I could stop myself. Coming down the stairs, say. More like a groan. We'd hardly ever argued. And that was what I started to do. Alone in the house. And I always ended up saying sorry. I sat with my phone on the table and I went through my contacts, looking for her sister, her mother, her father. I had none of them. Her friends – I could only think of a few. Three. A woman who I thought was called Máire, who went to school with her. A man called Colm who came out when he was thirty-nine – in our kitchen, in tears, in my dressing gown. And a woman I remembered because she's gorgeous. I looked at Laura's phone and I wondered if that was why she'd left it here; I'd go to her contacts and get the search party out, till we found her lying on a beach or in a river. Or, I'd phone and tell whoever was there that Laura was missing and there'd be silence, a delay, and I'd realise that I was alone, the only one who hadn't known the truth. Or, I'd open the phone and her contacts would be blank. But I knew: the phone was there so I wouldn't phone her. So I'd leave her alone. She was fine. The phone was saying. She was better off without me. No one else rang her, after I'd phoned, when I found the phone in the cutlery drawer. The battery went dead. I didn't recharge it. I left it on the table. And no one phoned me – none of her family. I assumed she'd contacted them. I'm thinking that now but I don't know if I thought of it then. I sat. For days. I stayed on the couch. I went upstairs to the toilet. I looked into the bedroom. I hadn't been in there – I worked it out – in three days. I went back into the bathroom. I brushed my teeth. I had a shower. I didn't shave. I decided not to. I put on clothes. I ate. I cooked. I ate again. All decisions. I went to the press under the sink. I got the Dettol spray and sprayed the table, and the keys and the phone. I sprayed the cooker, the counter, the taps. I cleaned the toilet, the bathroom sink, the shower. I put the sprays and the Toilet Duck back under the sink. I picked up the keys and phone and brought them to the cutlery drawer. I thought about recharging the phone, to check if there'd been any calls or messages. But I didn't. I put it back where she'd put it. I went out – it was late morning. I walked the 2K, and back. I took off the clothes I'd been wearing and put them in the washing machine. I went upstairs and put on clean clothes. I decided to start reading a book. I took one from her side of the bed. The thing is: I felt she was watching. I chose the one I'd seen her reading the night before she left. *Where the Crawdads Sing*. I didn't like it but that didn't matter. I watched the third season of *Ozark*. She watched me watching it. Not beside me on the couch. Somewhere else. She was watching me, on a screen, watching a show we would have watched together. I liked it, although I can remember nothing about it. Except that the lawyer, Helen, was too soft in this season. She wasn't as interesting or remotely as sexy as she had been in the other two, and then they killed her off at the end. The people who made the show were to blame – this was what I'd have said to Laura. They'd made her uninteresting, so she became expendable. I wondered if life was like that. Did we all make less of our partners, our spouses, before we walked out? I said it out loud, so Laura would hear me. Then that stopped. She stopped following me.

I went weeks when I didn't look at myself. I could brush my teeth squeezed between the shower and the side of the sink, away from the mirror. I approached the television sideways when I was turning it on. The screen would be full of other faces before I sat down to watch. I'd put my hand into the fridge, I'd see the hand and sleeve and – for a second – I didn't know whose hand it was, or whose red sleeve. I was wearing clothes that weren't mine; I hadn't brought them with me when I'd left. I hadn't looked at myself wearing them. I thought about Jim. But not often, and not after I knew I was well hidden. That seems wrong. I wasn't hiding. I wasn't frightened. He didn't push me out: I left. And not because of him. Because of me. Because of what I wasn't. And I did look at myself, eventually. I was rinsing the toothbrush, I knocked it off the side of the sink, it fell on the floor, I bent down, picked it up, stood – and saw someone. Me. That was it. I was there. I hadn't changed.

I looked out every morning and I hoped I'd see the car, gone. I'd have found it reassuring. It would have been contact. Stealing her own car – we'd have been sharing the joke. I didn't go to the Guards. I thought about it. But her phone and keys – the way she'd arranged them. She wasn't missing; she'd left. But I wondered if I was supposed to report it, anyway. What if she was found – a body, or she'd lost her memory – and the Guards called to the door? How long was it since I'd seen her? A week, two weeks, three, four, a month and a half, nine weeks. You have her phone? Yes. You contacted no one? No – yes, I didn't. I admit: it excited me, at times. The intrigue. We were doing this together – somehow. But I knew why she wasn't here. I knew why she'd gone and it didn't take me long to know it. She'd left – her decision. I'd pushed her – my decision. That's brutal, unfair – but it's true. But only true when I realised it. When I decided I wanted to do something, when I still felt that I was living in front of her gaze. I wanted to show her that I could act. Join in. Contribute. I was going to volunteer. I signed up to help at one of the Covid-19 testing centres, but got nothing back after the acknowledgement. I saw myself in the PPE gear, coming home, leaving the curtains open; she'd see me pouring a whiskey, bringing it upstairs to the bedroom and the shower. I was doing this to reassure her – I was doing it to prove to the fuckin' bitch that she was wrong. I was going to be fuckin' essential. I'd deliver food to the elderly, I'd organise webinars for those who were especially isolated. I'd see me doing this, and she'd see me doing it. But they stopped – the fantasies. I admit, they always ended with sex and not always with her, but she'd be watching. But it stopped – the revenge. When I thought of something I actually could do, that I was qualified to do. Listening to grief. Again, I saw myself. I had the headset on. I accepted the call from the bereaved. And I could listen – I could bring it that far. But I couldn't speak. My ears, my body, filled with someone else's anguish and I could offer nothing. I didn't know if the call had ended, if there was someone – man, woman, I couldn't tell – still crying. I knew what it must have been like for Laura. This is hard.

I stopped wanting babies when I was seventeen. I stopped thinking that I was supposed to be interested in childbirth and being a mother, experiencing a life grow inside me – any of that – my role, my future – any of it – when I was fucking Dean McAllister on his parents' bed. I was holding his hips, making him do what I wanted him to do and what he wanted too, and it was wonderful and so out of the world, I saw no connection between this and the future of the human race or my own future. Babies – children and the life that comes with them – I've never craved and I've never regretted. But not many people believe me, or let me believe. There was a while – years, most of my life – when I was made to feel like a freak because of it, or a slut or a liar or a woman who didn't know herself. There was a time when friendship was impossible, until I reached an age when it didn't seem to matter so much. A full hour could pass without mention of breastfeeding or the fuckin' Leaving Cert. If I sound bitter, I'm not. Now. When I moved in with Jim – and it's not very long ago – when my sister came to see where we were living, she stepped into the hall, past me, past him, and said, The last chance saloon – I like it. She had her brats with her. She has three but she's always managed to make it seem like more. Jim was convinced there were five. And they're lovely, by the way. But that was why the house was there, why Jim was standing beside me: to produce a baby before it was absolutely too late. I was thirty-seven. I'd told her – ten years before, fifteen years before, twenty years before – that I didn't want to be a mother, that I'd no intention of becoming a mammy, and she'd smiled and nodded the first few times, and laughed – I'm with you, bitch! – but she'd refused to believe me. I was tragic or perverse; I was both. I used to be her sister, until I didn't have children. So. All my adult life I've been a woman with no children. The witch, the weird one, selfish, barren, unfortunate. I've lived with three men. I left Frank because I stopped liking him and, while I was packing, I realised I didn't love him either and I couldn't wait to get out. We'd agreed that we didn't want children, until Frank's pal had one and Frank decided that he needed one too – I don't think I'm being unfair to Frank. He suddenly started to like romantic comedies. He discovered the godson he'd had for ten years. He brought the child with us to Paris; I should have paid more attention to the flight and hotel arrangements. I don't know if he has children now; I hope he does. The second, Felim – I left him after a month, when he pushed me. We were on the landing, close to the stairs. I don't think he wanted to send me tumbling down but I had to grab the rail, and I watched the same hand as he made a fist of it and, after the longest two seconds, I saw him loosen his fingers and he went into the bathroom. I was gone by the time he came back out. He'd pushed me – he'd thought about hitting me – because I wasn't his mother. She was dying; he was drunk. I was there. I cried for months, because I'd loved him. Really loved him. The last I heard – it must be six years ago – his mother was still alive, although I might be making that up. If there's one big love, the love of your life, that was Felim. Then Jim. We were sitting in the Light House cinema, at the same film, an empty seat between us, and when the film was over I heard him say, Was that shite? And I said, I kind of liked it. He burst out laughing, and so did I. He kind of bowled me over. He had his sad eyes but his mouth seemed to be in a battle with them, and when his mouth won he was lovely. And it was kind of lovely when the eyes were winning too. It was like watching the Battle of Britain. I told him that, when we were hopping between my place and his, and he loved it, what I said. We'll just have to hope the Nazis don't win, he said. He was an easy man to like. He held my breasts later that night, in his kitchen. He looked at them as he spoke: Never was so much owed, by so many, to so few. I definitely wanted to spend my life with him after that.

I was married before I knew Laura. The thing is, we had a child. A little girl called Susan. She died when she was three. A bicycle killed her. It wasn't one of the men in Lycra. I wish it had been – I could have done something with the rage; I could have tracked him down and killed him. But it was a girl. I've spent years trying to forget her name. She was cycling on the path; she wasn't going particularly fast. Susan ran down our drive. She didn't stop where we'd trained her to stop. She always stopped at the gate and held the middle bar. We left the gate open. And this time – the first time, I think. The only time. She kept going. The front wheel hit her. She was dead by the time Maggie got to her. We separated – I came here – ten months after that day. I haven't seen Maggie since the day I left; we'd agreed that I'd go first. I deleted her number and email from my contacts an hour after I shut my new front door. I don't know why; it just seemed the right, final thing to do. The clean break. I don't think I believe that now. Today, I'd hesitate. At least. I wish it had been me who'd shouted, 'Susan – stop!' I wish I'd been the one running after her. I wish I had that memory. I wish we'd been together. I didn't wish it then. I wished that Susan was alive but I seemed to accept that she wasn't, much sooner than Maggie. Maybe because I hadn't been there. I hadn't witnessed the split second. I never had to catch up with it –. I met Laura in the IFI – the Irish Film Institute. We were both at a film called *Upstream Colour*. She was sitting behind me and she kind of groaned when it was over. And – I don't know – I decided to turn and agree with her; I hadn't liked the film either. She laughed, and waited for me at the exit; she held the door open and said, Was that shite or what? I asked her if she wanted to go for a coffee and by the time we were out on Eustace Street we'd changed our minds about coffee and we went for a pint instead, in the Stag's Head. We went to her flat, via the chipper at the corner of her street. We shared a long chip, like Lady and the Tramp. I'm way too old for this, I said. You're never too old for chips, she said, and we won't be trying it with the cod. There was something about that – we were living together three weeks later. I told her about Susan and Maggie. I got that done – it felt like a thing I had to do – before she came to live here. Her eyes watered, I remember. And she hugged me. She moved in and we were a couple. One thing: we didn't speak about children. Neither of us did. I mean, children who didn't exist. Future children, possible children. They weren't in our plans. We didn't have plans. That was one of the things that I really liked about Laura. She'd no interest in filling in the future. I think it's true – I'd never met anyone like that. I don't know what happened. I do, but I don't know why – or maybe how. Because I fell in love with Laura; I really did. Her voice, her face, her sense of humour. The way she woke up, the way she held her fork. Infatuated is what you'd call it. And it was great, like years of my life had been bypassed. And that was the problem, too. Because the ten years – actually, eight years – were still there. Susan, and Maggie. I could delete Maggie from my contacts but I couldn't forget that I was the father of a child who wasn't alive. The father who'd left the gate open when he was going to work. Who, with his wife, had got out of the habit of shutting the gate, because their daughter was confident on her feet and she'd made a game of grabbing the middle bar and waiting for us to catch up. I'd be laughing with Laura and I'd see Susan's body on the path – even though I never saw her body on the path. I wasn't entitled to laugh. I don't think I thought this at the time – or, I don't think I thought as clearly. It never occurred to me to contact Maggie, phone someone who knew her, get over the embarrassment as I asked for her number, and phone her. But that's not true. It did occur to me.

And I didn't want to do it. Maggie was alive – the mess. Susan was dead. But alive – suddenly – because she was dead. I started to talk about her. I thought I was doing the right thing. And I'm nearly certain Laura thought so too. Maybe it was because Susan was so young when she died. Maybe because my heart and lungs, the things behind my chest, felt so colossal when I spoke; stopping became the hard part. I felt I was abandoning her when I stopped. I think that's honest. That saying, You can't be living in the past – I started to. But I made it up. I gave her a life she hadn't had. Or me. I don't know: I made an ad for fatherhood and climbed into it. Father and daughter, running together through rain, upstairs on the bus, gazing at the *Book of Kells*. I've never seen the *Book of Kells*; I've no interest in the *Book of Kells*. I'm sure I ran through rain with Susan, but I don't remember. I was filling in what I'd lost. And I was pushing Laura away. I knew it. But I couldn't stop. I brought Susan to school, even though she was too young to have gone to school. I knew then – that moment, when I started going on about standing at the classroom door, living some scene from a shite film I might have seen, looking in as Susan settled in and ignored me – I knew I was lying. But I cried. I missed the child in the classroom. I might have been lying but the truth in the lies really hurt. And soothed, too. Laura asked me if I wanted a baby, if I'd thought about it. Then she left. My fault. Entirely my fault. I'm not being sarcastic.

He'd told me about his daughter. It was sad. Terrible. It made sense of his eyes. But, to be honest, I was more curious about his wife. I wondered what she was like.

But I never said, Tell me about Maggie – how is she? He went quiet sometimes, withdrawn. But I liked that. He wasn't a mouth. I wasn't interested in rivalry; I wasn't going to make him happy, fuck all his sad thoughts away. He was who he was. I liked it when he talked about her. I felt trusted, I think. At first. Then – I'll be frank – it got boring. He'd start talking about something they'd done together. And this look on his face – he'd get this look. As if he was on *Sunday Miscellany*, or in a library telling a story to six or seven people sitting in front of him. He was different then; I didn't like him. We were driving somewhere – I think it was to my sister's. I was driving. And I saw it in the corner of my eye; he sat up and chuckled, and I knew he was going to tell me one of their adventures. I wanted to drive off the road. Or hit the brake and let whatever was behind plough right into us. It was unbearable. If I'd felt she was in the car with us, I wouldn't have minded. If it had sounded heartfelt – a decent story, I mean. But Jesus. So I said, before he got started. Listen, I said, do you want another child, is that it? It was brutal, I suppose. But it shut him up. That sounds brutal too. But I don't care. It was dreadful. I'm not a fool. If I'd let him keep going, he'd eventually have told me about his daughter's wedding day. Whatever about the psychology, whatever he was playing out or trying to do, it was boring. And it was nasty. He was the brute in the car, not me. I'd told him clearly – very clearly – once. Once was enough. I didn't want children. He knew that. I didn't want a child and I wasn't going to be pushed out of my own life by a madey-up one. I know that now. I was upset then. And confused. Guilty. Furious. Wrong. Lost. Lonely. And just about strong enough to leave. I've had to do that all my life, since

61

I made my choice. I've had to walk out of everything. That's the last time.

I was walking past a chipper, coming back from Lidl. There was a queue outside, so I had to go out onto the road, to keep the proper distance. But I saw a poster in the window: Staff Wanted – Deliveries. I stopped and went back – I was still on the road; there was no traffic. I looked in the window; the front of the shop is all glass. It looked the same as it always had, except for the perspex screen along the counter and the masks on the three people behind it, two men and a woman. I looked at the poster again. There wasn't a phone number or an email address and I wasn't going to queue. But I got home, found the Facebook page and phone number. I rushed at the decision. It was Mario himself, the owner, who picked up the phone and half an hour later I took the car key down off the hook beside the door. Mario gave me a bag of masks, and I bought a box of gloves and bottles of sanitiser, for the car. The area, it's mostly houses – one front door, one delivery. There are some apartment blocks but they're straightforward, with bells or buzzers for each flat. I didn't want to go in. I'd wait till the customer came down. But Mario told me I had to do it; there'd been a complaint. There were babies, disabilities, other difficulties. It was home delivery, so I had to bring the order to the door. And he was right. But some of the corridors, and even the lifts and stairs – they're a bit eerie. We'd watched too much Scandi noir, me and Laura. I half-expected pools of blood or dismembered bodies, or tall people in masks. I was wearing a mask, myself, and a woman screamed when she opened the door – and someone deeper in the apartment screamed too, and I thought then I'd interrupted the screaming, not caused it. She came running after me when I was leaving. I thought she wanted me to rescue her but she gave me a tip, two euro. Coming out of the place, back into air, whipping off the mask and leaning against the car – there were two snack boxes on the back seat – I decided not to go into an apartment block again. Until I realised that the encounter with the screaming woman had actually been brilliant. The things I see, the things I hear, and the silence, the suspense. But mostly, it's the gratitude; I just love seeing the faces. I ring the bell or give the door a whack, leave the brown bag in front of the door and step back. I wait till it opens, then wave. And the faces – whole families come to the door. They wave back, like I've battled my way through snow and wolves. They shout Thank You – two distinct words – because they assume I'm not Irish. I don't say anything. I'm behind my mask, the man of mystery. I love it – I absolutely love it. One thing, though: never assume that just because a house has one front door there's only one way of life behind it. I only catch glimpses. Sadness, poverty, slavery, savagery – there could be anything behind those painted doors. But mostly what I see is gratitude. In this lockdown a bag of chips has never been so exciting. And I deliver the excitement. I rang a bell. This was last night – this is fresh. I rang the bell, left the bag – scampi box, spice-burger and a Coke – and walked away, ready to turn and wave when I heard the door opening. I heard the click of the lock, and the woman's voice – Ah, thanks – and turned, and it was Laura.

*

I knew it was Jim before he pulled the mask down. Even though he looked different. His hair – it was longer than I'd ever seen it. And the beard.

How are you, Laura? I asked. Fine, she said. Good, I said. Enjoy your scampi box. I thought that sounded creepy, after I'd said it. I hesitated – I stood there. Only for a few seconds. Then I waved. Bye. I smiled. And went back to the car.

I called his name. He turned and looked at me. I like your Covid hair, I said. He smiled. He laughed. He put his hand up to his head – he was wearing latex gloves – and rubbed it. Thanks, he said. And went. He was looser – that was it. The way he moved, the way he was walking.

I stopped at the gate. I hadn't heard the door closing. I looked. She was still there. She was picking up her bag; she was looking at me. You're looking great, I said. Thank you, she said. She smiled and went back into the house. I should have mentioned her own hair – the bit of grey. It suits you. But I wasn't going to go back and ring the bell.

I knew I was okay. I knew: he wasn't going to come back or start looking in the window, or parking outside – in my car, by the way. Or leaning on the bell, pleading through the letter box. None of those nightmares.

He was the man I'd known out there. I didn't have to worry.

I was smiling when I got back into the car. And all night, I felt like a man who smiled readily. And I don't know why, really – because it's sad. Maybe because of the coincidence, delivering scampi to the woman who'd walked out on me. It *is* funny. And just seeing her – she was fine. But – I think it's this, why it's sad. All these things I've been seeing, this life I've been living – I wish I could tell her about them. I wish I was talking to Laura. But it's too late. There's no fixing it. She's where she wants to be. Maybe I am too.

It's sad. It is, in a way – in lots of ways. It's definitely sad. But everything's sad these days, I suppose. And I have to admit. I do have to admit – personally. I'm happy.

# Nurse

She sits at the table. She feels the back of the chair behind her. She needs it there. It's holding her up. She's afraid to sit back on the couch, to luxuriate, to let go. She's afraid to close her eyes.

She's not sure what's in the fridge. She's not sure if there's anything in the fridge. She can't remember this morning, what was in the fridge the last time she stood in front of it, before she left. She thinks she remembers milk. She thinks she remembers the carton being heavy in her hand as she put it back. She thinks she remembers a packet of tortellini. And half a banana.

She's not hungry.

She's starving but food would make her sick. Anything – it doesn't matter what – would feel uncooked and wrong in her mouth. It would choke her.

She'll have to eat. She knows that. She will.

She wants to phone her mother. But she won't – not yet. She isn't ready. If her mam asks her how she is she won't be able to answer. She won't say what she wants to say. She won't say anything that she feels belongs to her. She'll be out of control, not herself.

It's dark outside now. It wasn't when she sat. Although she doesn't think she's been sitting here for long. She can hear the usual noises. The children next door, on the stairs. It must be bedtime. Bedtime and early morning – that's when she hears them. She doesn't think they're speaking English. Shouting English. Screaming English. The fridge is ticking. There's a house alarm whining down the road. The noise has been there since she sat down.

She shares this place but it's empty, wiped clean, wiped lifeless. She'd love to see a mug. A bit of a mess. The other girls are gone, home. She's the only one who had to stay. Her phone is alive with alerts but she doesn't look at them. Looking would make her feel more isolated. And confused.

This is our Vietnam.

—What gobshite said that? her father asked her when she told him – last week, she thinks it was.

—Another girl, she told him.

—Don't listen to her, love, said her dad. —It's not Vietnam, it's no one's Vietnam. It's a hospital. I don't want to be harsh – is she a pal of yours, is she?

—Not really.

—Well, if she wants to pretend she's fighting the Viet Cong, let her. Tell her to watch *Platoon*.

She'd laughed. Her dad loves all the war films.

—Unless she thinks she's *in* the Viet Cong, does she?

—I don't think so, she'd said.

—Are you in your full metal jacket? he'd asked.

It's what he calls the PPE. All of his jokes come from war films.

—No, she'd said. —I don't wear it home.

Her face hurts, from the mask. It feels as if a branch sprang back and smacked her face. She's sure there are red marks across her cheeks. She won't look yet. Behind her ears is sore too.

Two people died today.

Joe – and Marie.

The zip on a body bag. It's not like any zip she's heard before. It was her first time hearing one, today, and watching the zip close over the chest, the face. Joe. He had to go into two bags – that's the procedure. They washed him. And they spoke to him. They told him what they were doing, even though he was dead. She said nothing at first, then she copied Áine, the senior staff nurse. We're turning you onto your side now, Joe. It was easier when you talked to him. No one spoke when Áine closed the first body bag. The rasp of the zip, like it was being pulled through wood – it's the last thing she'll hear when she closes her eyes. When she goes to bed.

She held the tablet close to Joe's face, so his wife could see him. Three hours before he died. She phoned her up and told her, two minutes after he died. You're great, his wife said. You're all great. She'd gone down to reception to collect a picture – a framed photograph of Joe with his wife and five children – that one of his sons had left there, to go into the sealed coffin with Joe. They won't be able to see him again. Four sons and a daughter. All adults. The daughter was gorgeous in the photo. Lucy. Joe told her the name. A week ago. She'd listened to Joe talking to his wife. Only a week. I'm alive, it's great. Each word was separate, a different effort. 'Great' took ages to come out of his mouth. But his face – he meant it. Lucy was pregnant. I'm the happiest man in the world.

She'll stand, in a minute. She'll go upstairs. She'll have a shower. She'll bring her clothes downstairs, put them in the washing machine. She'll look in the fridge, she'll eat something. She'll go inside and turn on the telly; she'll keep the sound down. She'll check her phone, make sure the alarm is ready for the morning. Then she'll phone her mam and dad. Her dad first. He'll make her laugh, and she'll cry. He'll listen and he'll tell her that he loves her.

# Masks

Ripped from his life, he walks. He hates it but he does it. He's been doing it for months. He's walked through the spring, through a summer he can't remember, and up to the edge of this winter. He's walked right through the year. He's added and subtracted the permitted kilometres, 2K to 5K to 20K, and back to 5K. He's kept to the same route. He's in the second lockdown and he's still walking between the sea and the road. He's looking at neither. He watches the sky and the people coming at him.

It's too warm. There are middle-aged men strolling in shorts and women swimming in the water opposite the yacht club. They're screaming but they're laughing. There are none of them suffering. They should be. It's the middle of November. They've been laughing since March. He hates them, with their dryrobes and the men in their brand-new wetsuits. He doesn't know them but he hates them. He walks into them, through them. He's alone. He's met no one he knows in the months he's been walking, to the end of his permitted distance and back. He's seen the same people – the men, the women, the gangs of teenagers – but he nods at none and none nod at him. He walks at them, never with them. He used to turn, in the early days, to see who might be coming behind him, walking his way. But there was no one. The crowds were coming at him, blocking his way. Like meteorites, or accusations, the opportunities and moments he's avoided all his life. They keep coming at him, out of the past. He keeps walking. His stride has its rhythm and it doesn't vary – my fault, my fault, my fault, my fault. It doesn't stop when he gets back to the house and sits, or when he lies down. The lockdown has ripped away the padding. There's no schedule, or job, no commute. There's nothing saving him.

The masks on the footpath disgust him. They lie flat on the ground. Most of them are blue. They don't make sense. The cardboard coffee cups are empty. So are the crisp packets. There are bins along the promenade, every hundred metres or so, but the usual rubbish – the cups, the plastic bags – make a kind of careless sense. The masks, though – they're diseased, vile. They're private. They're like underwear on the footpath, soiled and wet – or sanitary towels. He's walking through people who just drop their finished face masks on the ground.

He passes the wooden bridge to Bull Island. He passes the green-painted shelter where the man stands most afternoons and sings his arias. He doesn't look, he doesn't slow down. My fault, my fault, my fault, my fault. He passes the top of Vernon Avenue, where another man – a younger man – sits on the sea wall and plays the uilleann pipes, and further along a gang of girls from the school across the road sit on a bench and sing some song about feeling like an old cardigan under someone's bed. He doesn't look. If he could stop himself from listening, he would. So much life, so much

71

defiance. He can't stand it. But he strides through it, hacks through it, twice a day, four times a day.

He sang once. He often sang when he was a child. But this one time stands out. He remembers standing on a table, being picked up and placed there by his father.

—Good lad, up you go.

The wooden ceiling was right above him, touching his hair. He wasn't at home, in Dublin. He was in the big kitchen of his mother's aunt's house, the farmhouse in Wexford. He remembers adults and cousins looking at him. All talking and fidgeting stopped.

—Listen – listen now to what this young man can do.

He remembers this clearly. He opened his mouth and the notes and Latin syllables climbed from his throat in an easy line. He could feel them slide across the roof of his mouth. He gave them their shape and gently pushed them out. *Mari-a gratia plen-a.* They slid along the ceiling, down across the heads of cousins, around the shoulders of the aunts and uncles, his mother, father, his grandmother, neighbours, farmers, wives, more children. They sat on chairs and on the floor, the cold stone slabs. They all looked up at him, then at the notes – they were looking *for* the notes, the bits of Latin words. They were visible things, drops of glass – they had to be. *Or-a pro no-bis, or-a pro no-bis.* He loved being up there, while he sang and then in the moment after he'd pushed out the final notes and only he knew it. The silence, the two seconds of utter stillness – they were the best thing of his life. Fifty years ago. Feet stamped the stones when they knew he was done, farmers' hands hit the long kitchen table. Aunts wiped their eyes. Cousins slid on their bums to be nearer to him.

—He should be in the *Eurovision*, that fella.

—My God – whose side does that come from?

His mother's face, he'd never forget it. Joy, and terror. She was afraid of what was up there on her aunt's table, and of what was going to happen.

—We'll be giving the boy a big head – he'll be getting notions about himself.

It wasn't his mother's voice. She wasn't the woman speaking; that was one of his aunts. But the words, their meaning, were on her face. He wanted to get down. He wanted to be her boy again.

She's long dead. There were other nights and days when he sang. On tables, chairs, in corners, on a stage. When he sang and his mother smiled back at him, and smiled more when he stopped. Then his voice broke. He doesn't know if he can hold a tune. The adult – the man – has never sung a song.

He's at Vernon Avenue again. He walked as far as the traffic lights at Castle Avenue, and turned. He stays inside the 5K. 5K out and 5K back, to the empty house he's lived in all his life. Twice a day. The girls who'd been singing when he passed the first time are gone. The man – a boy, really – is folding his uilleann pipes into their case. The tide is out. It's getting dark. The lights along the promenade will come on soon. It's still warm. It's still busy. There's no rush for home. The lockdown's a nonsense. It's more crowded than it ever was before the pandemic. There are chip bags and empty snack boxes all across the grass and footpath. And the masks. Dozens – hundreds of them. They're damp and lethal on the concrete, like the leaves.

He bends and picks one up. It's wet. The white straps for the ears are still intact. He puts it on. He pulls it over his mouth and nose. The cold is pleasant on his face, and behind his ears. He feels grit on his lips. There's another mask in front of him. It's another of the blue ones, just thrown there. He picks it up. He puts it on over the first. He feels the two masks pushing into his skin. There's water running down his neck. He's killing himself but he picks up another. Someone else's discarded droplets – he pulls it over his face. He can feel the weight now, pulling against his ears. He sees a black one, an elegant one. He picks it up. He notices something as he surveys and roams the wide footpath. He has it to himself – he sees no other feet. He looks, and sees people looking at him, huddled, keeping their proper distance for the first time in months. He decides – it delights him: the black mask is a cap and he puts it on top of his head. He bends and gathers up three masks. He puts one strap over his ear and the other around a button of his shirt. He pulls another across his forehead. He lifts his hands so he can place the third one across the back of his head. His head must be getting bigger. The thought makes him laugh. He keeps adding the masks. His bending is effortless. He adds layer to layer, mask on top of mask. He can still see. People are out there – he can see them, just about. He stands under the light, just come on. He stands right beside the lamp post. It's silver-painted, beautiful, probably Victorian. He takes his final mask, a leopard-skin thing that's much too small. He holds it up and out, shows it to the crowd – and brings it quickly to his eyes. He hears a gasp – a woman standing nearby. The straps hold. His ears are really sore now, both sides of his head. He's in pain. It's as if he's being held up off the ground by his ears. He keeps his hands close to the sides of his face, in case the straps

74

begin to slide or snap. He can see nothing. His head is huge – it must be. He can't breathe. There's a point, a hole, a gap, below his cheek. A kink in the first mask has created a narrow cave. He can suck in air and pestilence. He sees absolutely nothing. But he's looking out at the audience. Someone laughs, then someone else. He hears a clap, a big man's hands. And another clap – applause.

—Well done!

—Well said!

—Brilliant – fair play to you.

He's art. They think he's art.

—Oh, God, he hears, a woman to his left. —Listen – listen. He's singing.

# The Charger

Mick looks at what he knows he doesn't see. And he sees it. He looks away, and looks again – and still sees it.

He left the phone charging beside the bed. He left it there most of the morning. He stayed downstairs, well away from it. He's noticed, particularly since this thing started, how he takes the phone everywhere with him, how he keeps checking for emails and messages and WhatsApp things. He's noticed as well the disappointment, the little devastations, when there aren't any messages. He's putting distance between himself and the phone.

He was the last man he knew to get a mobile. There was once, before Mary bought it for him – it must have been twenty years ago – he'd missed the ferry from Holyhead. He was going to have to stay there, in Wales, till early morning and the next boat, and he spent half an hour looking for a payphone that worked and then another twenty minutes gathering up enough coins to phone home, buying chewing gum in one shop to break a fiver and a packet of Polos in another, to make coins out of a second fiver. It was raining, pissing down like it only ever did in fuckin' Wales, and he phoned home, water crawling down his back, and he realised that it was much too late to be calling. He could see Mary sitting up in the bed, worried. He could hear the twins waking, and their new sister. He was going to hang up when he heard Mary.

—Hello?

She sounded frightened. He told her it was him and he told her he'd get a mobile phone, before he told her that he'd missed the boat.

—Are you alright, though? she asked.

—I'm wet.

—For fuck sake, Mick.

—I know.

—You could have texted me.

—I know.

—You'd have been able to text me. If you had a bloody phone.

—I know. I'll get one – I will.

—I'll do it, she said. —I don't trust you. It can be your birthday present.

—It can in its hole.

—They're not cheap.

—Okay – fair enough.

—See you tomorrow.

—Yeah.

—Are you drenched?

—Yeah.

—Serves you right.

—Did I wake you up, by the way?

—Are you jestin'? Say hello to your daddy.

He ran out of money before the girls had finished shouting.

The phone he has now – another present from Mary; she keeps buying him phones – is too big for the side of his head. You could go to Mars on the fuckin' thing.

His daughters gazed enviously when they came home and saw it.

—It's only a phone.

—Ah, Dad –.

It has seven apps he can use and two hundred he's never tried. He can check on the football scores, bet on the odd horse, and pay for his parking. When he does that, when he sits in the car and arranges the payment with a couple of taps – he feels a bit proud. But it's only a fuckin' phone and he's sick of what it's doing. He keeps checking, constantly looking at the screen. When he thinks about it, his hand is already in his pocket, hauling the thing out. He knows already; there's nothing.

But it isn't just the phone. It isn't the phone at all. He's losing it. His grip, his mind. Whatever it is – his life. His hands shake. He sees that when he goes to pick up something. Milk from the fridge or the fuckin' phone. That's one of the attractions, he thinks – the weight and the shape of it in his hand. It keeps him rooted, stops the shakes. He wakes with a house brick sitting on his chest. He sleeps on his side but wakes on his back, the weight of the brick immediately there, a big dusty breeze block; the corners dig into his ribs. His eyes are so dry, especially late in the day, it feels like he has the eyesight but not the eyes, just red-raw sockets. Noise comes at him from everywhere. The fridge's sudden growl, the cistern filling, everything threatening to break or explode, to fill the house with water and shite, flood the place with failure – Mick's.

He isn't essential.

He said that to Mary a couple of months ago, when all this was still new.

—Ah, you are, hon, she said, and she fucked him later to prove it.

—Well now, she said. —That was fairly fuckin'
essential.

She burst out laughing and pulled him into it,
wouldn't let go of him till he was laughing like he used
to, big booming guffaws that bounced around in the
dark of the bedroom.

That was months ago. Mick doesn't know what day
it is, and can think of nothing that will pin him to his
place in the week. He knows it's a weekday, that's all.
Today – the thing he's standing in now – means nothing. He's awake; that's all.

It's not true: he knows exactly what day it is. Today,
of all days.

There's no one who needs him. That's not self-pity;
it's fuckin' great. Or, it was. There was a moment, a
year ago maybe – less, more, it doesn't matter; a good
while before the pandemic – he was standing in the
kitchen and he'd nothing to do. It wasn't tasks he lacked;
it was responsibility. All four girls were gone and earn-
ing, his parents were dead, the house was paid for.
There was nothing that needed doing, no one to look
after.

—Except me, said Mary, when he told her.

—Well, yeah, he said. —But you know what I mean.
Don't you?

Mary liked these conversations, the tricky ones that
strayed from the usual. Mick hated them, but he liked
watching Mary get worked up, popping up with things
that startled him, reminded him of who she was and
why he loved her.

—It's the third age, Michael, she said.

—The wha'?

—Your third age, she said.

—It has a fuckin' name?

79

—If you want it.

—I don't.

—The golden years, Mick, they're all ahead of you. Cruises, cyclin' – you can go to fuckin' Trinity if you want. You're always readin'. Do a degree.

—I don't want any of tha' shite.

—You said – a minute ago, Michael. You said you could do anythin' you wanted.

—Yeah, he said. —But that's it.

—You don't want to do anythin'.

—Kind of – yeah.

Another thought hit him, and it was a relief – the cavalry.

—An' anyway, he said. —I haven't retired or anythin'. I have a job.

—But you've reached a point in your life – look at me, Mick. I'm talkin' to you. You've reached a point – a plain. A plateau. After a lifetime of hard work.

Mick has been working since he was sixteen.

—All I said was – I'm glad the kids have fucked off. That's all.

—That's not all, said Mary. —Fuck off now, Mick – admit it. You were devastated when Allie left.

Allie is their youngest and she was the last to pack her bags.

—Okay.

—I was the one who was delighted.

—Okay.

—But you're ready, she said.

She put her arm across his shoulders. She's a tall woman.

—You're goin' to ask me to cut the grass, he said.

She laughed.

—Ah, Mick, she said. —The grass is grand. The grass can look after itself. It's all ahead of us. Decades of bliss. And – tell us.

—Wha'?

—Do you ever think about what I might want?

—Honest to God, he said. —I don't mind cuttin' the grass.

That was – when was it? – less than a year ago. A couple of months of freedom, not much more. Half a year exploring the land of not giving a fuck. He can't imagine it now, that state of mind.

And now this.

The phone isn't where he left it earlier, on the floor beside the bed. He steps back, nearly out of the room, and looks again. The charger's there, plugged in, but not the phone. He pats his pockets again. Jeans, shirt – he knows they're empty. It should be there on the floor, where it isn't.

There's something else.

He listens. He knows exactly who's in the house. Himself, and three of the girls. Daisy works in Super-Valu, up the road. She's gone from joke job to frontline worker, overnight. They've sent their daughter off to the front. She brings home the stories. Their biggest worry for years – the sleepless nights, fuckin' hell – Daisy has become the best part of their day. When Mick hears the front door, when he hears Daisy climbing the stairs to wash her hands, he wants to whoop. In the early weeks, when it was all a bit of an adventure, it felt like the last anxiety had been lifted; the plague had brought them contentment. Even though Daisy is inhaling strangers' droplets all day, putting her life on the line to keep the neighbours in pasta and toilet paper, they aren't afraid. They love what their girl has become.

He was looking out the bedroom window – he's doing that a lot. He was looking out, down, when he realised he was watching Daisy coming home from work. She dropped her cigarette on the ground, stood on it, then took her mask from a pocket – Daisy never carries a bag – and put it on, over her mouth. He watched her put the elastic behind her ears, watched her pull the cotton – her mother made the masks – over her nose, before she took the last few steps to the front door. She was letting them see that she was wearing the mask, before she took it off. Like a kid. It delighted him. The life in the dishonesty, the humour. The willingness to compromise. They'd reared her well – he can believe that. Or, he could, back when it started.

They've been locked in for months. For more than two months now – he thinks it's eleven weeks. There's himself and Mary, and the four girls – all of their children are girls. He's loved the words, since the second and third girls, the twins, were born – 'my daughters'. The girls were in the lockdown, committed to the thing, like Mick and Mary. They came home for it; they abandoned leases, friends, lovers. The first weeks were lovely. Now, though, in the middle of month three, on the edge of June – it's hot; it hasn't rained properly in ages – they come and they go. He envies them their secret lives. Della looks up from her phone, say, and announces she has to water a plant. She gets up and she's gone for days. There are no looks between the girls and their mother, no nudging or banter. He loves their secret world. He wishes he had one of his own.

Which one of them is trying to kill him?

It's mad, that thought. He shakes his head. He actually does – he shakes his head to get rid of it.

Mick knows nothing about electricity. He remembers a scene from a film, when a toaster was dropped into a bath. He can't remember the film but the fact of it, the toaster dumped into the water, was outrageous and brilliant. He remembers women screaming and laughing all around him; he must have seen it in a cinema. He knows these things are dangerous, the toaster, electrical goods in or too close to water. But he doesn't know why; he's never found out.

He has few memories of his father. The man died when Mick was eight. There was a day, though – he remembers a day when they went for a walk. It's just the two of them in Mick's head. The road became a country lane a few doors down from their house, so Mick and his father walked out of the suburbs into County Dublin, rural Ireland. His father held his hand – Mick remembers that. He took Mick's hand after a few minutes, not to stop Mick from straying or because they were walking through crowds; they weren't. He held Mick's hand because he wanted to. The garden walls became hedges. A few years later the hedges were gone and the road had been widened; there were houses in the fields. But not that day. Mick must have been on that stretch of the road before but his father led him to a place he'd never seen and never saw again. There was a gate, wider than a farm gate, and a smell that didn't come from animals or new-cut crops. It was like petrol, the smell. It was tar, his father told him, as he picked Mick up and let him hang on to the gate so that Mick's head was at his father's shoulder. Mick saw piles – pyramids of wooden poles. The poles were on their sides, five or six thick, high triangles of them. They were all perfectly straight; it was hard to believe that they'd once been trees. There was a shed, probably a Nissen hut – Mick's memory doesn't really include the hut, just the fact that it was there, and locked. The poles were pylons, his father told him. For electricity. For all the houses that were going to be built soon, along the roads that were going to be laid. The tar was creosote, his father said; they covered the pylons with the creosote to preserve them, to stop the rain from rotting them.

—I like the smell, said Mick – he remembers this.

—Me too, said his father. —I always have.

—Why are they wooden, Da? Mick asked.

—The poles?

—Yeah.

—Because wood doesn't conduct electricity, his father told him. —The electricity can't run through it – can't travel through wood.

He pointed at the wires above them.

—The poles keep it up there, safe, he said.

—Is it dangerous? Mick asked.

—Electricity?

—Yeah.

—Oh, it is, said his father. —It's good stuff but it's lethal.

That's all. The memory stops. For ever, Mick's face is at his father's shoulder and they're looking at the wooden pylons that were going to hold the electricity, safe, above the heads of all the people who came to live in the new houses.

Now, Mick is looking at an assassination attempt but he doesn't know how it's supposed to work. The charger is in a bowl of water. He'll be blown across the room. Because water conducts electricity, but he doesn't know how, or why. He'll be dying stupid. There's so much he doesn't understand. He's gone through life not knowing things that others seem to know. He sits with the girls and Mary in the kitchen and he listens to them talking about the virus and he feels like he's at a press conference; they're all specialists and he's a thick who can't think of a decent question to ask them.

Electrocuted. That's the word. Up his arm, across the room. The smell of him cooking will bring them up the stairs. He looks: there isn't enough space for him to be blown across. He isn't in a film. His side of the bed is three feet – half a social distance – from the window. Would he go through the window – would the charge be strong enough to send him through the glass, leave him on his back on the roof of the car, or in next door's garden?

Who did this? Did someone get into the house? He's been downstairs all morning. The side gate was open because he'd brought one of the girls' bikes around to the back of the house. The back door wasn't locked. Did someone sneak in when Mick was looking elsewhere? It's not impossible. It is, though; it's mad. Who out there would want him dead? Who'd give a fuck if he's dead or alive?

The bowl he's looking at, it's one of their white cereal bowls. There are three left that aren't broken; there used to be six. The bowl is where the phone was, where he left it earlier this morning. There's water in the bowl and the charger – the tip, whatever it's called, the part that goes into the phone – is dangling in the water. The skinny white flex is hanging over the side of the bowl. He expects what he's looking at to change, to turn into what it should be. It's a trick of the light, it's where Mick is standing. The phone will be behind the bowl, the bowl will be empty, the bowl will be something else, a sock or a T-shirt. But it's one of the bowls from the kitchen and the working end of the charger is swimming in it.

They want him dead. He isn't surprised. This is mad, too – he knows it's mad. It's as daft as the thought that someone crept into the house to do this. His phone isn't where he wants to see it, so his wife and daughters are conspiring – there's another great word – they're conspiring to murder him. They want the funeral. They'll all speak well; they'll tell funny stories about their dad. There won't be a proper funeral, though; it'll be one of the pandemic rush jobs. Maximum of ten, close family only, ten minutes in the church, no gang in the graveyard, no soup and sandwiches, no pints or singing after.

He's useless.

He sits on the floor.

There was the incendiary device a pal of Mick's made – way back this was, during the Troubles, when you'd hear things like 'incendiary device' and 'hunger strike' and 'Diplock courts' all day on the radio. Mick thinks he was in second year, in secondary school; he was fourteen or fifteen. One of the lads, Mungo Loftus, sat up when he heard the reporter on the telly say the words 'a simple device', and he did a bit of homework. He went to the new library in Raheny and he asked his uncle the electrician a few innocent questions and, inside a week, he'd made a car bomb. They stood around Mungo – Mick and the other lads – at the back of the last of the building sites, and Mungo explained what he'd done. He was gas, Mungo. Mick has no idea what happened to him, or where he is; he isn't even sure his name was Loftus. But Mungo showed them the coffee can, and the fertiliser – the stink of it – and the thing that looked like a cassette tape cover with the wires going in and out of it. This, said Mungo, is our electrical initiating system. Mick hadn't a clue what Mungo was talking about; he'd stopped trying to keep up. He'd never know how Mungo managed to set fire to a digger – blew the fuckin' thing up – while they lay on the side of a ditch and watched. There was a fizz, then a roar that rolled at them, then what sounded like metal buckling and the digger – already a muck-covered red before Mungo's demonstration – was engulfed in flames and it wasn't a joke any more. They were climbing out of the ditch when the digger exploded and the ditch turned inside-out – Jesus Christ.

What a thing to carry, what a great fuckin' story. Mick had been there, he'd felt the earth open, he'd felt his bones shake, he'd felt the dirt rush at his face. But he'd never understood it. He'd never been able to explain how Mungo had managed the timer, how the electricity had come into it. The story had always been incomplete.

And it still is. He doesn't know what can happen. He doesn't know what has happened. He's clueless. How has it come to this? How has it come to what?

It's eleven weeks – he thinks it's eleven weeks. Maybe twelve. Before that, before the lockdown, the virus had been in the news but it had nothing to do with them. It was over in China, it was over in Italy. Then there was a case in Ireland – a case, not a man or a woman. The case got off a plane from Milan. The case was on a bus from the airport, to Busáras, then across the street to Connolly and onto the train, the Enterprise, to Belfast. They'd laughed, him and Mary, as they listened.

They've been saturated with information for months now, a solid chunk of the year – although it feels like much more than a year. The last of his aunties has died. He'll be getting some money once whatever it is – her house – is divided amongst the nieces and nephews. She'd told him at a wedding – he can't remember who was getting married; it wasn't him – that he'd be getting a few bob when she died. She'd been like Marlon Brando in *The Godfather* that day, the way she waved at the nephews and the nieces, calling them over, telling them the lucky news and warning them not to tell anyone else. Anyway, she's dead. Mick wasn't one of the ones selected to go to the funeral. He'd watched it on Mary's iPad. But the point is: he knows the virus killed the poor oul' one but he doesn't know how. After hours, probably days of experts and diagrams, he doesn't really get it. Mary knows, Mary understands. And the girls know. But not Mick the thick. A persistent cough, sneezing, a fever, a headache – you're on your way. A bad heart, bad lungs, diabetes, too much weight – you've a one-way ticket to ICU. That's his knowledge. It took him the first month to get into his head what ICU stood for, exactly. He's stuck in a world he doesn't understand.

He's being hard on himself. He knows as much as he needs to know. He won't pretend he's an epidemiologist, like half the fuckin' eejits he meets when he's out on his 2K walk. He's always hard on himself. He knows that. And it doesn't stop him.

He'll get up and look closer at the charger and the bowl.

The fragility of the world is the biggest shock. He doesn't think the last recession, the big one, was anything like this. It was bad but – fuck it – he could go for a pint. There was a different kind of social distancing. There was the fear when someone's name came up on the screen as the phone rang. *What does he fuckin' want?* Questions were dangerous. Get-togethers were scary, until you saw the faces on the men and women you were meeting. Mick knew one lad who'd definitely killed himself and another who probably had – his car had gone into a wall.

This, though – this is so different. He can't see himself walking into a full room again. The heat, the sweat in the air, the steam, manoeuvring himself through bodies to get close enough to shout for a pint. Putting his hands on the counter. Picking up a wet glass. Pulling open a packet of crisps. Licking the salt off his fingers. It's not going to happen.

He'll never stand in a pub again – he doesn't care. He's done something. He doesn't know what. Or maybe he hasn't done something – noticed something. Whatever he was, whatever he had – it's gone and he missed it going. The pubs can open – in July, August, next year; he doesn't know – but he won't be there. He doesn't even joke about it. He can't. He's talking to no one. He's shut down. He doesn't know how, but something must have happened. Because his family – the women – want to kill him. There are no other candidates in the house, unless it's Mick and he can't remember.

He'll stay where he is for a while. He has the room to himself, even if it's a booby trap. He can hear the water tank above him, filling. Someone's having a shower – again. He's lain awake listening to the tank. He never really noticed it before, the hum, gurgle, the pause and return to the hum, as if the tank has stopped for breath.

There was once, a few years back, he came into the house. He heard what sounded like a distant scream, and running water, nearby – too near. He looked into the living room and saw water pouring onto the carpet. Onto the coffee table, onto the couch, sliding down the wall, behind the family photographs. He was still trying to see it, to accept what he was looking at, when the ceiling – the plaster – collapsed. He remembers being upstairs before he was aware that he was going up. He went straight to the bathroom. He turned off the tap, the screaming stopped, and he could hear the gurgling he's listening to now, the tank filling, the pipes trying to keep up with demand. What he saw was only a trickle, climbing over the lip of the sink and sliding down the pedestal, under the lino he'd put down himself, back when he was the father of one child. The catastrophe downstairs in the living room and the trickle of water up here – the floor wasn't even wet; the gap in the stories made no sense. But the house had been empty all day. He'd been the last one out. He'd left the fuckin' tap on, and the plug in. The end of the world downstairs was his own doing. The water had slid down, through the thin gap between the base and the lino, through the gap in the floorboards, a trickle, a pool, a reservoir, held for most of the day by the living room ceiling. He sat on the side of the bath till he remembered the name of the insurance company, and he found their number and spoke to a girl called Fiona who told him she'd be his case buddy until everything was sorted and – it's true – he felt happy. Fiona told him she'd email him some forms, and he was putting his phone back in his pocket. He was thinking about what he could do now, immediately, when he heard a slight groan from a floorboard as he stood up off the bath and the thought hit him: he was standing on floorboards that were soft and rotten and if he moved now, if he as much as budged, he was going to go through the floor and the bath was going to follow him. But this – this is what he remembers, what he still feels in him: he laughed.

Now though, the pipes and the tank – the same pipes and tank – drive him demented. The tank is fine. The constant hand-washing, hair-washing, dishwashing, clothes-washing – it's nothing to the tank. But the noise is eating into Mick's head.

He listens.

He can a hear a voice – it's Kat – and little, cracked voices under hers. She's having a Zoom meeting in her and Daisy's bedroom. He can't make out words but Kat's doing most of the talking. There are people in there, in boxes on her screen, listening to his daughter, and making sure they look like they're listening. It's amazing. Her job description is made up of three words. Project and Manager; he can't remember the third – actually, the first. Area, or Regional, or National. Or it might be Creative. Anyway, one of his girls is in charge of a gang of people in there. She's doing a job he doesn't understand. But he doesn't mind that one, not understanding; he's proud of that one. He put the side of his head to the door – not long ago – and tried to hear. But the other doors on the landing were shut and they all seemed about to burst open, to expose him snooping, spying, creeping around his own fuckin' house. His ear against the door seemed to make him deaf. He got away, downstairs, outside. He stood in the garden. For an hour.

He listens. The neighbours are new. New in that they only moved in last year. And new in that they're young; their kids are tiny. A little girl and a littler boy and, now as well, a dog. There are more dogs around than a few months ago. Dogs just getting the hang of themselves, yapping away, as if they're rehearsing. He's seen them when he's out. Dads and kids teaching the new dogs to be dogs. He's stood out the back and heard the names – Colin, Max, Arthur. Human names. The dog names seem to be gone. Mick had a dog called Buster when he was a kid. There'd been a dog up the road called Dog. Their own dog – the dog they'd had when the girls left – was called Crystal. She died in the second week of the lockdown. Mick, first up that morning – most mornings – found her in the kitchen, at the door. There was something about the way she was lying, the way her head was out of place – she wasn't sleeping. He'd wrapped her in a couple of old sheets and left her outside and he'd cleaned up the mess that must have been her last protest by the time Mary, then the girls, came down and he told them. He'd called the vet and brought poor Crystal to the vet's door and knocked on the glass till the vet, a nice young lad, a vet with a ponytail, opened the door, already wearing the gloves and mask, and asked Mick if he had Revolut on his phone because he wasn't taking cash and he didn't want to use the card machine. Mick told him he'd sort it when he got home and thanked the vet and he was back in the car before he remembered to have a last look at the dog; they'd had her for more than ten years. A great dog – she'd watched the football with Mick and barked whenever he shouted. He misses her. Now – he does. They laughed that night at the dinner, when Mick pointed out how right it was that the vet would have a ponytail.

—He identifies with the animals.

—I've never seen a pony in the waitin' room.

—Maybe it's the aspiration, said Mick. —It's what he wanted to be.

—A pony?

—No, he said. —Racehorses an' tha'. He wanted to work in that world. The trainers an' the millionaires – the fuckin' Aga Khan.

—You might be right.

—An' he ended up with dead dogs on his step.

—Ah, Dad.

—Poor Crystal.

Mick was in charge of that conversation, and it's not that long ago. It's months, not years. He's the same man, surely. The girls were upset, Mary was upset, Mick was upset. But he'd made them laugh; he'd made a good night of it. They got a rubber band out of the cutlery drawer and made a ponytail for Mick, with the bit of hair he still has at the back, and they photographed him – his profile – and sent it off to fuck knows who or where. Only two months ago. That's another app he has on the missing phone. Revolut. Daisy showed him how to use it, and he fired off the money for Crystal's cremation. Very straightforward – a bit too straightforward. It's the only time he's used it.

He'd love another dog. He feels that, at least. He'd love a dog. If he had the phone he'd start looking at dogs, see if there were any rescues inside the permitted five kilometres.

He lies on the floor. There's a shoe under the bed. A man's shoe. It isn't his. It is – it has to be. It looks weird, though, alone. There's no sign of the other one. The shoe's too far back to reach. There's a book too, in against the wall. It's twisted looking, buckled, as if it's been wet and has dried too quickly. The dust – it's a landscape under there. There are dunes. You could

93

play golf under that bed. The thought pleases him. He can imagine himself saying it, performing it – being Mick. There's something else under there. His phone – the fuckin' phone. It might be the phone. There's another shoe, an old espadrille Mick brought home from Portugal – no, he bought them in Marks & Spencer's before they went.

—Typical Mick, Mary had said. —Why don't you buy the fuckin' wine before we go as well? And a sombrero.

The summer before last that was. When the grass turned brown and they forgot what rain felt like, they went to the Algarve and got pissed on for two weeks. It's the same this year. Right through the lockdown, it's rained about twice. The grass isn't growing. It's hot when he wakes. He wore the espadrilles yesterday – he thinks he did. That's why they're there, at his side of the bed, where he parks his feet. That might be the phone there, behind the espadrille, close to where he left it. Exactly where he left it. He doesn't want it. He doesn't want to pick it up. He doesn't want to know he's looking for messages he hasn't been sent. He's more himself, here, on the floor. If Mary comes home he'll pretend he's unconscious.

He'll tell her he's listening to the rug's confession. He'll tell her he's looking for his phone. He'll tell her he's miserable, he can't stay upright.

He sits up.

She isn't in the house.

He'll stay where he is for a while. He doesn't want to see the bowl. He doesn't want to accept that his head is playing tricks. The tricks make more sense. The assassination attempt – it makes him feel wanted. Or noticed.

Jesus.

Mick wants nothing to do with Mick. He's been crying. Not now – he's grand at the moment. He remembers crawling under beds when he was a kid. He did it all the time – he was famous for it. He fell asleep under his aunt and uncle's bed and the Guards were called before they found him.

He could still hear his mother.

—If your father was here –.

—He's grand, he heard his uncle. —It happens to all of us.

—When was the last time you slept under the bed? his auntie asked his uncle.

—Under the bed, on top of the bed, said his uncle. —What's the difference?

—There are significant differences, said his auntie.

They'd already forgotten that Mick was there – his Auntie Una and Uncle Albert.

Mick spent the holidays with different aunts and uncles. After his father died – Mick has no memory of the funeral; he's not even sure if he was at it. He just remembers the big empty thing in the house. His father. The hole that never filled again. His mother hated crying. I'm an eejit, I'm an eejit. Mick remembers her sitting at the kitchen table, wiping her eyes, almost like she was pulling them out. I'm such an eejit. She got a job in Cadbury's and Mick went to his aunts' and uncles' houses when the school was shut for the holidays. He was the youngest, the only boy. He slept on floors, he slept in rooms full of cousins who didn't want him there. Albert was his favourite. Albert and Una didn't have children; Mick was alone in the house with them. Una followed him around with a wet cloth. She tried to smile. She stood beside his chair while he ate his dinner. She gave him ice cream and Angel Delight; she came home from town with a T-shirt for him, with Batman on it. She held her hand to her mouth as he put it on. It was the best thing Mick had ever been given and she couldn't see it. He felt like he was acting – like he was lying – when he told her he loved it. Albert was sitting in his chair. He lifted his paper up over his head and looked under it. He was always pretending he couldn't read properly, even though he was always reading. He looked at Mick and read Mick's chest; he squinted.

—Fatman, he said.

He looked at Una, he looked at Mick.

—There isn't a pick on you, Michael.

Mick laughed. His eyes filled. He cried. He stood in his Batman T-shirt and cried and felt himself disappearing, turning into nothing. And Albert's hands were on his shoulders.

—Better out than in, Michael – better out than in.

There was a hankie under his nose and he could smell his Auntie Una's soap. He cried into the hankie. He can feel it now, decades – a lifetime – later, like the mask he wears when he goes into SuperValu. The same thing, the cotton, the feeling that he was choking. His uncle was telling him to cry, his aunt – she didn't know it – was telling him to stop. It was the only time he cried, the only time he remembers. Until now, the pandemic months, the last few weeks.

There was a time in school. He thinks he was fifteen; he thinks he was in third year. There was no teacher in the room and Mick and some other lads were messing. He can't remember what he was doing – it was nothing dramatic – but a teacher looked in from the corridor, stepped in and pointed at Mick.

—You –.

96

And at four others.

—You, you, you and you. Out here – now.

The teacher, a cunt called Fallon, prowled the corridors looking for victims. When the other lay teachers – the ones who weren't Brothers; the Brothers had their own room – when they were in their staffroom, probably eating buns and talking about the women teachers in the convent up the road, Fallon wandered around with his leather strap in the inside pocket of his jacket. Where other men put their wallets, this cunt hid an instrument of torture. He lined up Mick and the other boys outside on the corridor; he didn't explain why he was doing it. Three of the best on each hand. By the time he got to Mick, the perspiration was running down Fallon's face and neck, into his collar, and when he lifted the strap to bring it back down hard – so fuckin' hard – on Mick's open hand, drops of the man's sweat – fuckin' droplets – landed on Mick's face. He can still feel it. The strap landed on his palm and he thought he was going to die. He couldn't believe his hand wasn't broken – that would have made sense.

—The other one – come on.

Fallon was talking to him. Mick dropped the thing, the meat that used to be his right hand, and held out the left. It started again. He groans – Mick groans, now. Nearly fifty years later, Mick can't recover, can never really recover, get back to where he was before he went out to the corridor. But he didn't cry. That was the important thing. That sweat – Fallon's sweat – spraying onto Mick's face. Mick knows now: he was sexually abused. In a school full of men. On a busy corridor. But he didn't cry. He was in agony; he would still be shaking when he got home six hours later. He'd hold the metal legs of his desk; he'd clutch the legs, so the cold of the iron would pass into his hands and soothe them. Was that conduction? he wonders now, the cold passing into his bones, the heat of his pain going into the iron legs. His palms were still sweating when the last bell of the day went and he bent down to pick up his schoolbag. He leaned down – he remembers this; he feels it – and he wasn't sure he wanted to straighten up, stand up; he wasn't sure he could do it. He wanted to fade, to melt away across the floor. He grabbed the bag and stood. He hadn't cried. That – still – was what mattered. He'd walked back into the classroom after the beating. The teacher was in there by then, writing on the blackboard. He must have walked past Mick and Fallon to get there. Mick walked to his desk, and sat. He saw the faces – nearly forty of them – his friends, and others. He looked at them; he fuckin' smiled. He sat and stopped himself from vomiting. His pal beside him, Quackser, wrote down Mick's homework because Mick couldn't hold his pen. That was the day, the moment – Mick still thinks this: he knew he was a man. He'd passed. He left school at the end of the year, maybe three months after Fallon attacked him. He didn't cry.

In Una and Albert's kitchen, he'd cried – six or seven years before Fallon got him. He cried and he couldn't stop. The hankie was up against his nose, his mouth. He felt Albert's hands on his shoulders, and he heard him.

—It's great havin' you here, Michael, he said. —Isn't it, Una?

She didn't hesitate.

—Yes, she said.

But the next holidays, the next summer, he was sent to a different house.

He told Mary about it.

—You were fostered, she said.

—Was I?

—Yes, Mick. You were fostered out.

—Well, said Mick. —Like. What does that mean?

Could a charger dangling in water kill him – when he went to lift it out? He's seen pictures before, burn marks on mattresses after chargers had been left on them, after a power cut or something, when the power came back – surged. That's another word – surge. Varadkar had used it in his speech on St Patrick's Day. He'd said there'd be a surge. He'd been talking about death, the virus rolling through the population. Leaving people dead on the side of the road, Mick thought, like during the Famine. Mounds of bodies. Doused and torched, to stop the spread of the plague. That was nearly three months ago, and it hadn't really happened. There'd been no surge. Because they'd washed their hands and stayed inside. They're still alive. No one too close to Mick is dead, except for the old aunt. He never knew her well. He was never sent to stay in her house during the school holidays. But the other surge – he's seen the scorch marks on mattresses and on wooden floors, on Facebook. He knows: if phone chargers were dangerous there'd be no one left alive. If they wanted to kill him they wouldn't be using a charger. There's no one trying to kill him.

He'll stay here for another while.

He remembers sliding under the bed with one of the girls – not this bed. It was Della. It was her bed, in the room she's probably in at the moment. He'd seen her feet, her white socks sticking out from underneath, as he was going past the open door. He went in.

—I'd know those feet anywhere, he said. —What's the story?

He bent down and started to tickle one of her soles.

—Daddy – stop!

He stopped.

—What're you doin' under there?

She was ten, maybe younger. A great kid, a wonderful kid – a brain he could never catch up with.

—Remember the smell? she said.

She was still under the bed.

—I do, yeah, he said.

There'd been a smell in Della and Abbie's room, a bad smell, a dead-mouse-behind-the-skirting-board-but-don't-tell-the-girls smell, about a week before, for three or four days. It became a joke until it wasn't there any more. But Della had managed to find it.

—What's under there? Mick asked.

He hadn't looked yet.

—Me, said Della.

He remembers. That moment, that syllable – *Me* – he was so happy. So content. So sure of himself. He sat on the floor, at her feet.

—What else?

—Come and see, she said.

And he did. He got down, turned on his stomach and slid under the bed to join Della. There was enough light from the window to brighten the patch of floor before them. Della was looking at a very dead mouse.

—It's a mummy, she told him. —But it's different.

—How is it?

Up close, it was stinking, fuckin' minging. But Della wasn't interested in the smell.

—Mummies, she said. —Do you know what mummies are, Daddy?

100

—Mummies an' daddies?

They laughed together under the bed.

—They're the Egyptian things, said Mick. —The bodies o' pharaohs an' tha'.

—And cats, she said. —We went to see them in the museum, do you remember?

—Yeah, he said.

—They're preserved for thousands and thousands of years, she said.

She was whispering.

—In the pyramids, he whispered back.

—Yeah, she said. —But this one will only be preserved for a little while.

—How d'you mean?

—He's a mummy now, she said. —But soon he'll be just a decomposing mouse again. Probably tomorrow. I was lucky I found him today, wasn't I?

—Very lucky, said Mick. —An' so am I. What'll we do?

He could feel her breath on his face. She patted his hand.

—There's no need to do anything, she said. —He's dead.

He was being given a lesson in biology, mortality. The mouse was a tiny thing, fading away.

—Don't tell the others, Daddy, she said.

—Okay, said Mick. —Why not?

—We'll let him rest in peace.

—Grand – okay.

There's nothing dead under this bed here. As far as Mick can see. Except maybe Mick. He isn't though; he's here – he's alive. Della – he's thinking of little Della. What a child she was. What children they've all been.

—You were fostered, Mary told him.

—I wasn't put into a home or anythin', he said.

—No, but you were sent away.

—What else could she have done? Mick asked.

He really didn't want to hear a good, straightforward answer, a list of the options his mother had dismissed in her rush to get rid of Mick.

—I don't know, said Mary.

They were at a table outside a restaurant in Majorca. He can't remember the name of the town, a small place that didn't seem to have anyone under the age of fifty, unless they were carrying plates. It was their first child-free holiday since the honeymoon.

—Maybe nothin', said Mary. —I'm not criticisin' your mother, Mick.

He nodded.

—I'm not, she said.

—You used to, he said. —Sometimes.

—Yeah, she said.

Mick's mother was long dead.

—But I'm not – now, I'm not, said Mary. —How come I'm only findin' out now?

Mick had been telling her about Una and Albert.

He shrugged.

—I don't know, he said. —Like – I didn't know you didn't know. It wasn't a big deal.

—It was a huge fuckin' deal – excuse me. Don't fuckin' deny it, Mick. I'll get up now an' I'll walk straight back to the airport an' leave you here on your own if you deny it.

He smiled.

—Listen, she said. —Listen. Your mother rejected you. Here's the starters – perfect timin'.

They watched the waiter put the plates in front of them. He was taking his order pad from his apron pocket as he turned away. There was a table of Brits shouting for him. Mary lifted her glass.

—Come here, she said.

She waited for Mick to pick up his.

—She wasn't the worst, she said.

They tapped glasses.

—Ivy.

—Ivy.

—Poor Ivy. But Mick.

—Wha'?

—Only hearin' this tonight, said Mary. —I'm furious – for fuck sake. We're married –. How long are we married?

Mick was better with dates.

—Twenty-six years.

—Twenty-six.

—It's easy, said Mick. —Just remember Della's age – it's the same, most of the year.

Della was born four months after the wedding.

—Is that how you remember it?

—Yeah.

—Are the kids more important than the weddin'?

—The weddin's just a date, said Mick. —The girls are the girls.

—Jesus, Mick.

—Wha'?

—When you talk like that I just want to go over there and put my cock in your mouth, she said.

They exploded. Even the Brits looked over at them. There was a little piece of Mary's starter on Mick's shirt. He'd seen it coming at him. He knew it was there but he didn't look down at it – he made sure he didn't.

He remembers they walked down to the promenade, after the food.

—It's lovely, isn't it?

—So's Howth.

—Ah, fuck off.

He remembers they were holding hands.

—So, why did you never tell me? she said.

—It was just –, he started. —It was just the way we were organised after my father died.

—You didn't hang around with your friends durin' the summer?

—It depended, said Mick. —Tommy an' Vera – another aunt an' uncle. They lived near us – not too far. An' I had me bike. So –.

—What were they like?

—Grand, said Mick. —Like, they were all grand, really. But they had six o' their own. I can't even remember all their names. But they didn't want me there. D'you know the way the girls used to fight for our attention?

—Used to?

—Well, they didn't need me there, gettin' in their way. The poor little bollix with the dead da, takin' their parents' attention away from them.

—How many years?

—Six or seven, said Mick. —Seven.

—God.

She squeezed his hand.

—Last time, Mick, she said. —Why didn't you tell me?

—I didn't know I hadn't, to be honest.

That was true. To an extent. He hadn't been aware that Mary knew absolutely nothing about what happened after his father died. But that must have been the case. Because Mary had a filing cabinet in the back of her head. She remembered all of that stuff. The human stuff. Mick could mention someone he'd worked with years ago and Mary would remember that the chap's wife had a miscarriage just after they got married. That would be the thing that mattered.

—These years, she said that night. —You told all the funny stories about your family.

—They *were* funny, said Mick.

—Some of them, she said. —But – like. I always thought you just had a big family.

—I did have a big family.

—Mick, she said. —You didn't have a family at all.

—That's not true.

They were still holding hands.

—It is, she said.

Mick – then, there, on the promenade in Majorca – agreed with her. He was afraid to breathe. He was afraid he wouldn't be able to. It was out. It was there – as they got to the place where the crowds came at the same time every night, to see the sun drop into the Mediterranean, right between the port's two piers. His shame. The truth inside the funny stories. They stood in the crowd – maybe thirty people. Couples like Mick and Mary and a few hippie-ish kids, and two middle-aged lads – Mick was betting Danish, and gay – in yellow Lycra; one of them was holding both of their cycling helmets. They watched the red sun bleeding across the surface of the water. They'd done this every night. They'd three nights left. That was his shame, he thought – the red ball, sinking into the sea. He inhaled – he managed that. And he exhaled. He was grand. He was better. He was different. The shame was still there half an hour later; it hadn't sunk with the sun. And the sun would be back in the morning. But it was different. It was there. He was unloved, unlovable. Unwanted. That was who he was. What he was. What had happened.

—Did nobody see? Mary asked him when they were sitting outside the hotel with two gins that were just a small bit cheaper than the flights home.

—See wha'? said Mick.

—*You*, Mick, she said. —Did nobody see you properly? You must've been fuckin' miserable.

He shrugged. He couldn't help it – it was done before he could stop himself. But he made himself speak. He made himself say the one true word.

—No.

—No?

—No one saw.

—They didn't want to see.

He shrugged again. This one was honest, though.

—The cunts, she said.

—I thought it was normal, he said.

She looked at him. He looked across at the low wall that hid the drop to the beach and the sea. He looked at her.

—I still don't believe, he said.

—Believe what?

—That you love me, he said.

Her eyes filled. His didn't – he didn't cry.

—I mean, he said. —I do. But –. I don't deserve it. That's what I mean.

—Mick –.

—I keep –, he said. —This is true. I keep expectin' to be sent away.

—You've been waitin' – what was it – twenty-six years?

106

He looked at the sea wall. He nodded.

—Sorry to disappoint you, she said.

She sighed.

—I'm stuck with you now, she said. —Just to prove you wrong. Your fuckin' mother –.

He grinned. She was saying something – your fuckin' mother, *my* fuckin' mother – he could never have said. Speaking on his behalf.

That's five years ago now. It must be five years. They'd loved it there; they said they'd go again. He can't remember what the fuckin' place was called.

He'd told himself: he'd talk like that again. To Mary – again. Openly. He'd let her know. He'd give her insights into the man she thought she was married to. Regular insights. One a week. I wet the bed till I was sixteen – did I ever tell you? One of the aunties – her brother felt me up, did I tell you that? For crisps and a can of Fanta. To counteract the funny stories he'd told her and the girls, for years. The four boys in the one bed, the dog on the motorbike, the uncle who came in drunk one night and farted 'Strawberry Fields Forever'. That was Mick's favourite, because he'd made it up. It had never happened. One of the girls – he thinks it was Abbie; he knows it was Abbie – had discovered the Beatles. Mick heard 'Penny Lane' when she was standing beside him in the kitchen, when she was putting the lunch she wouldn't eat into her schoolbag. She had her earphones in – the buds, whatever they're called – but he could still hear it, a hint of it, enough to tell him what it was. He'd made up the story later and they'd believed him. It's still a thing in the house when there's a smell that isn't welcome. They'd been in stitches earlier – earlier in the lockdown, months ago – when Kat had told them about a meeting – a real meeting, in a room, with people – when someone had farted and Kat had gone —Strawberry fee-ilds foreverr, before she'd had a chance to think about where she was and what she was doing. All six of them around the table pushing the tears back into their eyes with the backs of their hands, touching their faces, rubbing the infection into the sockets – doing exactly what they weren't supposed to be doing. Delighted to be there, loving the isolation. Because of a story Mick had made up years before. That was the type of father he was – *is* – the type of man he is.

Mary isn't here. Mary isn't in the house.

The time has come. Mick gets up off the floor. He needs the side of the bed to help him. He's stiff. One of his legs is half-numb. He leans on the wall and kicks the blood back into it. Gives the leg a shake. Tries to laugh. Something to tell Mary. He puts the foot on the floor – he's fine. He takes a step – he's grand. He sees the bowl. It's empty. The shift in the light, the angle of the sun. How long has he been here in the bedroom? Not that long. Did he fall asleep? He touches his face, feels around his mouth for the slobber of unplanned sleep. There's nothing – he hasn't been sleeping on the floor. But the bowl is empty. There's nothing in it. Except. Now he sees what it is. There's a line around the inside of the bowl, about halfway between the bottom and the rim. Dried milk, he supposes – congealed. Mary must have been eating – he stands right over the bowl – Weetabix, it's Weetabix. She was eating it while she was getting ready earlier, before she went. That line – it's hardly there now but the line of the milk looked like the extent, the height of the water he thought he'd seen. The charger – he sees now – the cable curls but the charger part, the jack or whatever it's called, is behind the bowl. And the phone is exactly where he left it.

He doesn't know what's happened. He's relieved – and he's not. He's – he doesn't know what he is. He's a nothing. An emptiness. He's a place where a man used to be. He sits on the bed. He leans down, picks up the phone. He doesn't look at it – he decides not to. He leans back, lets it fall onto Mary's pillow, Mary's side of the bed.

She isn't well.

There was just themselves. And then there was the lockdown and the girls were dashing back to the house. And it was great – Mick can still feel that. They'd looked at each other, him and Mary – what the fuck was going on?

He got into the bed, later that first day.

—How long will this go on, d'you think?

She knew what he meant.

—Fuck knows, she said. —It could be months.

—It's kind of nice.

—That's what worries me.

They lay together and listened to the girls downstairs, repossessing the house. He kissed the back of Mary's neck. She pushed herself gently against him.

—They're watchin' *Gilmore Girls*.

—Jesus, he said. —How many episodes?

—There's over a hundred an' fifty.

She was gone – her arse at his stomach was gone.

—Where're yeh goin'?

—Just gettin' me phone, calm down.

—Why?

—To text them to turn it down, she said.

—I can't hear anythin', he said.

—That's the next thing, she said.

—Wha'?

—You're gettin' your ears tested straight after the fuckin' lockdown.

It had been like Christmas, with the girls home. Except for the hand-washing and spraying the front door and the letter box, and the fear that it was still going to get in – on his shoes, in his breath, that he was going to carry it into the house. The surge. They'd all watched Varadkar together, on St Patrick's Day. They'd sat and listened. No one said a word. Varadkar was good. Mick was glad he was young – he wasn't sure why. He looked healthy. They'd listened, and they'd gone their separate ways and still ended up in the kitchen, all together, a quarter of an hour later. They'd stayed in there for days. That was what those early weeks felt like. He was the father of daughters again, in the role – the hopeless dad, the funny dad, the dad who came in and looked at them and walked back out, the dad who kissed their foreheads. But it was different – it *is* different. He isn't that man at all. That man isn't needed. His wife has disappeared. He doesn't know what to do.

He leans back, picks up the phone. He checks: no texts. She's out there, in the virus. She had to go, this morning. What time is it? She's been gone for hours.

She's gone to the Mater Hospital. She put on her mask and went out to the taxi. He watched from the window here while she leaned into the taxi and wiped the back seat with one of those Dettol wipes, while she straightened and looked back, up, at him – she knew he was there – and got in, and went. She's gone for a check-up. It's much more than a check-up. He doesn't know why she's gone. She didn't wave when she got into the taxi. He's glad she didn't; she wasn't saying goodbye.

He's nothing without her. That much he knows. He has to get a grip. He has to be standing up when she comes home. He offered to go with her, to bring her; he offered to drive. He wanted to go with her. He's reminding himself – he wanted to do the right thing. But the virus wouldn't let him. She had to go alone. She couldn't bring anyone. If she has to stay – if they find something – she won't be allowed any visitors. That might be the last time, when he stood at the window – that might be the last time he'll see her. It's not impossible. She hasn't texted. He checks again; she hasn't. He gets up. He goes to the window. No sign of a taxi. She said she'd text.

He doesn't know what's wrong with her. That's the problem – that's *his* problem. She's told him. He's listened. But he can't hear. He hasn't been able to grab hold of words. He'd take it, whatever she has. He'd take it out of her – the tumour, or whatever it is or might be. He'd put it into himself, swallow the fuckin' thing whole. It should have been him getting into the taxi. He doesn't exist without her. She'll be grand without him.

If – say she phones now and says they're keeping her in, if he gathers the girls to tell them, and one of them asks why, he won't be able to explain it. They'll know already; she'll have told them. They have the information that he can't keep hold of. His wife became sick; something happened – and he doesn't know what. It's a blank fizzing-white wall – that's his mind. It burns anything that goes near it. Words shrivel. Nothing stays.

He made a list. It's in his phone. He tried to get the words down, to keep hold of his wife. Just the medical stuff – that was what he wanted. The terms – a few names. What colour are her eyes? He thinks they're brown – she's fading already. She's in pain, surrounded by people in full PPE gear, strangers made even stranger. She needs him – he can see her hand reaching out.

He'll go down to the kitchen. He'll do things. He'll make sure he's occupied when she gets home. She can't see him up here, staring out – where she left him hours ago. Like a kid waiting for his mammy to come home. For fuck sake, Mick. He'll go out; he'll go for a walk. She'll be here when he gets back. That wouldn't be right, though – that would be heartless. If they still had the dog, the walk would be justified. The right thing to do. The thick bastard of a dog, dying when it did.

He's out of the room. He's on the landing. He goes back inside and gets the bowl. And back again for the phone.

That night, the night in Majorca, she held him. Back up in their room, after all the talk. She pulled him close – she nearly hurt him.

—You're here, Mick, she said.

She grabbed the sides of his face.

—I'm lookin' at you, Mick, she said. —I'm lookin' straight at you. D'you know why?

—Why?

—Because I want to, she said. —Because I fuckin' love you. You're my man, Mick. Fuck them. Bastards. You're my man.

It's Mary's turn. He has to look at her. He has to hold her. It's her turn – it's his turn. She has to see him looking. She has to hear him. It's up to him.

He's on his way down. If the dog was alive, Mick would check that it wasn't lying across the top stair, nearly the same colour as the fuckin' carpet.

—We'll need a new carpet for the stairs, he said once, soon after they got the dog – years ago. —Either that or you'll be a widow before you want to be.

—No, Mary said.

—Wha'? said Mick. —You want to be a widow?

—It's a pleasant thought, she said. —But no. Did you never notice?

—Notice wha'?

—Everythin' in the house ends up the same colour as your dog.

—Even us?

—Even you.

He's thinking of that – he knows he's smiling – when he hears the car outside. He's sure it's a taxi. The air has changed since the lockdown started. Mick hears children he didn't know existed, he hears birds he's never seen, he hears bike wheels turning, people talking a street away. He hears Dublin's insects – there's billions of them. He hears the car stall, he hears a delay – he does; he can hear the delay before a door opens. He knows it's a back door, and it's the one beside the kerb. He hears a heel, he hears the taxi driver laugh. He hears the car door close. He hears Mary walk to the gate. He hears the driver hesitate, looking at Mary walk away before he starts the car. He hears her on the drive, he hears her dress brush against the side of the car. He hears her heels on the porch tiles. He hears her search for her keys in her bag. He hears her give up. She's going to ring the bell. He's ready. He brushes the dog hair off his shirt. Dead for months but the hair lives on. He'll tell her that, when they're in the kitchen. She's on the other side of the door. He'll open the door while her finger is in mid-air. She'll scream and they'll burst out laughing.

And that's what happens. Exactly that.
He opens the door.
She screams.
They burst out laughing.

# The Funeral

The last days had been hard. The last day, the day of the funeral, had been very hard. The Irish do funerals well, they say. Death doesn't frighten the Irish. They know all the right words. *He was a legend, a saint she was, a saint, he did great things for this place, I'm sorry for your troubles, I used to love meeting her, he'll be missed around the town.* They know how to sing. They know how to get drunk. They know how to stay polite for the day. If there's genius, if there's a national flair, it's in the ability to get rat-arsed and remain civil and cute, to let go and hold back. To wait.

Except for one fuckin' eejit.

Bob was awake.

There hadn't been a proper funeral, and he hadn't been at it.

He wasn't the fuckin' eejit. That was someone else.

His wife, Nell, was asleep beside him. He was in his own bed. It shouldn't have surprised him – he'd been nowhere but home for months. But it did surprise him. He listened to her breathing, the slight, lovely snore. He found his phone where he always left it. Under the pillow, under the edge nearest his side of the bed. He'd slept all night. There was daylight across the ceiling.

115

The traffic was missing. There were no cars passing outside. The lockdown quiet.

There wasn't a hangover. He'd earned one; he remembered that. He'd been drinking for days. But he felt great. Free, somehow – and clear. In his lungs, in his head. He'd get up quietly. He'd make the coffee, he'd scramble eggs. He'd stick on the radio; he'd take in the news. Precise bits of Covid-19, the stats, the new language. He'd get back into the life.

He was drunk. Still drunk. Lightly drunk. Ballet dancer drunk. He was at the bottom of the stairs before he knew he'd been on the stairs. The descent had been effortless. More than that – miraculous. Forgotten. Weightless. He checked the man in the dressing gown. It was him. He looked back up the stairs. He'd come all that way. His sore shoulder wasn't sore; the pinched nerve had gone away. He was in the kitchen. He threw open the fridge door. It felt like weeks since he'd looked inside it. There were one, two – there were seven cartons of milk. There were tomatoes. There was half a lemon. There were eggs – there was a box. There were eggs in the box – five eggs. He was up and running.

His phone hopped on the counter. He grabbed it. Afraid it would jump onto – *into* – the gas, under the pot he'd just put there for the eggs. He lifted the pot, dropped the pot, singed the sleeve of his dressing gown. Boy, he was drunk. He could smell the cotton, if it was cotton. He could smell something else, something important. Hair – he'd singed the hair on the back of his hand. He turned off the gas. He checked again – he'd turned it off.

It was the fuckin' eejit. The name on the screen.

—Bob – that you?

The fuckin' eejit he'd never have to see or listen to again. Ever. The fuckin' eejit he'd pinned to the wall of the church the day before – only yesterday – in the rain. But he wasn't sure about that detail. He didn't remember rain. He put his hand on the dressing gown, on his chest. It wasn't wet.

He didn't wear the dressing gown to the funeral.

There'd been no rain, and he'd pinned no one to the wall of a church – there'd been no church. He was making up something that hadn't happened. There had been a funeral but he hadn't been there.

—Don't call me again, he said now, into the phone.

He put the phone back on the counter. He looked at the singed hair. He held it up to the light coming through the window. But there was no real light.

It was dark out.

But there'd been daylight upstairs, at the gaps in the curtains and across the ceiling. It was why he'd got up. It was why he was in the kitchen. He looked at his watch. It was five o'clock, ten-past five. He looked at his phone. It was ten-past five there too. He'd been asleep for three hours. He was still in yesterday. Still drunk, still not at the funeral. His mother was still dead.

Fuckin' hell.

There were three stools at the kitchen counter. He sat on one of them. He felt the heat from under the pot. He got up and turned off the gas. He'd turned it off already; he knew he had. But it was on and he turned it off – again. He smelt the hair, he looked at it. It was like ash on his hand, on the back of his hand. He swept it away with his other hand. It was gone. He was hairless. There was no trace of it in the air. On the floor. On the front of the dressing gown. He turned on the light over the hob. He sat.

Coffee. He could smell coffee but he hadn't made any. He got up. He filled the kettle. He sat. He held on to the counter as he lowered himself.

His mother was dead. It wasn't a new day yet. He was stuck in her death. God love her. The bitch. The messer.

—I won't be naming you in the will, Robert, love, she'd said. —I thought I should tell you first.

He was an orphan. A big fuckin' orphan. And the other big orphan had phoned him at five in the morning. The phone bounced again. He looked at it. He picked it up. He tapped the green button. Missed – tapped.

—Fuck off.

He stood up, he put the phone in the fridge, he sat down. Hands on the counter – the kitchen stopped rocking. He heard the phone in the fridge. He laughed. A phone going off inside your fridge was pretty fuckin' brilliant. Fuck, he was drunk. He looked around for the mayhem, the evidence. The empty bottles, or the overturned furniture. But there was nothing. The kitchen was the way it was every morning. Nell must have tidied up. He looked at his hairless hand. He was still drunk. But he wasn't. He was fine. He breathed deep – he was great. He could go out now and drive. He'd be grand with the gear stick, and his feet on the pedals. He knew he would. It would be easier than making the scrambled eggs – and safer. A quick buzz from inside the fridge. The dope had texted him. Hilarious.

He wouldn't drive. He could but he wouldn't. He had nowhere to go. He was confined to the 5K limit. He was where he wanted to be. With his family above him. His wife and two of the children, home for the lockdown. He couldn't smell the hair now, or the dressing gown. He wanted to tell Nell about the hair. He'd make the coffee and bring it up. He'd tell her, then he'd come back down and do the scrambled eggs. Scrambled eggs on toast. On a tray, up to Nell. It was five in the morning – he couldn't do that. He'd let her sleep. They were all exhausted. So was he. He was tired – he had to admit. He felt it now. He'd go up and join Nell, get in beside her. Sleep again. He wouldn't sleep, though. He was up, awake. Stuck between now and yesterday. Between his mother and her death. She was with O'Leary in the grave. She *was* O'Leary in the grave. O'Leary née Considine. In the grave beside her husband, the big O'Leary. He hadn't seen her go in. He'd been barred. Banished. From his own mother's funeral. From his own mother's death.

He lifted his hand and walloped his chest.

—Orphan!

And it was her fault. The eejit in the fridge was only her lackey. The dope. *I won't be naming you in the will, Robert, love. I thought I should tell you first.*

That was one of the poems he'd had to learn for the Leaving Cert. *United Ireland's dead and gone, it's with O'Leary in the grave.* Was it 'United' or 'Romantic'? It didn't matter – he couldn't remember. But the slagging he'd got because his own name was O'Leary. They'd decided that United Ireland was the name of a porn star. At the back of the classroom, and on the bus home. A tall blonde with bandoleers crossing her chest and green Doc Martens. The lines they'd made up for the film. *Fuck me now*, buachaillí – *you can come on my thirty-two counties.*

That was where he could go. The grave. He'd drive there now. Say hello to his mother. And his father – he kept forgetting about his father. He had company now, in the grave. The graveyard would be locked but he'd get over the gate or the wall. If he was stopped on the way – if there was a Garda checkpoint at the bottom of the road – he'd tell them where he was going, and why. They'd let him through, drunk or not – his mother was after dying, for fuck sake. This was Ireland, not fuckin' New Zealand. He'd tell his mother why he hadn't been at her funeral. She knew that already, though. She'd rigged it that way. But he'd go anyway. He'd lie on the grave, lie down in the muck. One last bawl for the mammy.

W. B. fuckin' Yeats.

He'd arise and go now, he'd get into the car, say good-bye to his mother, then drive somewhere to watch the sun coming up. That would be good. Howth – the top of the hill. The Summit. The car park up there. He'd done that before, now that he thought of it. Him and a girl, in his first car. They'd watched the sun rising, from – was it the east? It was definitely the east and it was spectacular that morning. It must have been, because he'd asked the girl to marry him. Thank Christ, she'd laughed.

—Cop on, Bob.

—Serious.

—Fuck off.

Mary, Mary, Mary, Mary, Mary – not Mary, Sandra – Sandra Crosbie. Mary was her sister.

—We're great together.

—Together?

—Yeah.

—Who got the blowjob, Bob? You or me?

—Me.

—Correct.

—It was a bit more than a blowjob.

—It was a bit less than a fuckin' marriage proposal. You don't want to marry me.

—I do.

120

—No, you don't, Bob.

And then – the way she was speaking to him and looking at him – he absolutely did. He wanted her with him for ever. Teasing the fuck out of him. Sandra. It was definitely Sandra. His phone was hopping again, in the fridge. The grave, then the Summit car park – sorted. He'd go now. He was off.

He tripped over the dog. The dog was right at his feet – the fuckin' thing must have been *on* his feet and he hadn't noticed. He was grand, he was okay – him and the dog. He'd landed on his knees but it wasn't full-bang, or whatever. It was more like he slid across the floor. The dog came with him and they stopped, together – Torvill and Dean – when they hit the dishwasher.

—Alright?

He was talking to the dog. He did it all the time – they all did. But this time, just for a second, he waited for the answer. He grabbed the dog.

—Come here, you fuckin' eejit.

The dog was a fuckin' eejit, another of the fuckin' eejits. A great dog, though. And the way he could disappear, make you forget he was there, could stay so still you forgot you had a dog – it was impressive. It was evil.

He hugged the dog.

—You're a gobshite – what are you?

He couldn't remember the dog's name. He couldn't remember the name of his own dog. Jim. The dog was called Jim.

—You're a gobshite, Jim.

He'd get up now.

He was up.

He waved a bit, he wobbled. That was the blood pressure – he had low blood pressure. Sometimes. So he'd been told. Better than high, he'd been told as well. He wasn't going to fall over. He'd have a drink. Before he went to the graveyard. But he'd gone through all of the Jameson. There was no sign of a bottle, on the table or the counter. He'd been drinking for days. There was a can of craft beer in the fridge. That would do him. He'd drink it now. One for the road. It was too early for sobriety – it was still yesterday.

He opened the fridge. The door always put up a bit of a fight. The bit of resistance. There was no beer – he looked behind the cartons. Where he knew he'd seen one. He took out his phone. Two texts since the last time he'd looked. He put it back, on top of the Dairygold tub. And saw the can. On the top shelf, in front of his eyes. Underdog. From the brewery in Kilbarrack. Very nice. And three sausages, wrapped in the plastic, in behind the can. He took them down as well.

He'd make a coddle. He'd make a real Dublin coddle. He'd throw in a few chillies, make it a bit exotic. They could have it later. He dropped the sausages into the empty pot that was already on the hob. They'd have it for the dinner, all of them together. The smell of it would fill the house all day. An announcement. Normality's back, Dad's making his famous coddle. He looked down at the sausages. He'd never made a coddle in his life. Neither had his mother. He put his face in the pot. They smelt okay, the sausages. He coughed. Right into the pot. He laughed. Into the pot. He could feel the sausages, the grease of them, the life in them, on his skin, his cheeks, like the tips of fingers. What else went into a coddle? He'd boil the sausages in the Underdog. A new type of coddle. A Covid coddle. He opened the can. He put it to his mouth, sucked up the froth. Then he poured most of the lager in on top of the sausages. He looked around. He tried to remember where the onions were. And the carrots. If he found one, he'd find both. He tripped over the dog.

—For fuck sake, Jim – good man.

He saw the onions and he saw the carrots. Over, beside the back door, where they always were, in the stack of red plastic baskets. It was all coming back to him, the dimensions, the distances. His home.

The chopping board – that was what he needed now. And the good knife. He'd have to cut – chop – the onions. The state he was in, there'd be blood in the coddle. No harm. The iron would be good for them. He had the knife and he had the chopping board. The smell of the cut onion. It was liquid in the air, wetting his face, his eyes. He wouldn't be crying. He was a Viking. He was betting the Vikings threw in human blood when they first came to Dublin and invented the coddle. He could see a Viking running a blade across his thumb and letting the blood fall into the pot. He was laughing now, snorting. He definitely wasn't crying. That would be a good one for the telly – *The Cooking Viking*. Shouting the ingredients from the back of a longboat. *And bloot!* He'd grab a slave and hold him over the cauldron, cut the poor lad's throat. *Must be young!* The recipe would be up on RTÉ's website, or in the *Guide*. The thumb would be better, scarier, somehow – the Viking slicing his own thumb as the boat broke through the waves. He wouldn't even look. He'd be staring at the camera as he cut, no grimace or grin. *Ten seconds!* And he'd hold the thumb over the pot as he counted them out, in Danish or Icelandic.

He slid the onions off the board into the pot. Big slices – segments, really.

He'd wash his hands, give them the full twenty seconds. Sing Happy Birthday twice, he'd heard someone on the radio say when the whole thing had started, when his mother was still at home. When he'd still been able to see her. When he'd still been allowed to. When he hadn't been banned by his brother, his sisters, the fuckin' state. And his mother.

He was looking at the carrots. They were cleanish already. He'd cut off the ends but he wouldn't bother peeling them. They'd turn to great mush in the pot. They'd be swimming in the Underdog and falling apart all day. He bit into one. The crunch – the fuckin' Viking. They didn't make enough of the Vikings. The fact of them, the legacy, the blood. You lived in Dublin, you were a Viking. That was that.

He heard the phone in the fridge. Another text. No – it was a call. His brother was in his own kitchen. Doing nothing useful.

The phone stopped ringing.

Bob's mother was dead.

The energy was gone. He didn't want to cut the carrots. He couldn't drive to the graveyard.

—I won't be naming you in the will, Robert, love. I thought I should tell you first.

His mother had set the trap long before the pandemic.

—You were always the independent one, she'd said.
—You never needed anything – always on your own.

She was in the hospital, the first time – it must have been three years ago. He was sitting beside her. She was sitting up. He watched as she ate a pot of yoghurt, left over from her lunch.

—I remember saying it to your father, she'd said. —Whoever that fella belongs to, it isn't us.

There'd been fights when he was a kid, a teenager – and later. He wouldn't go to mass, he wouldn't take advice, he'd batter his way through his own mistakes. *We're your parents*, he remembered his father saying, shouting it, after he'd told them that he wouldn't be going to college. *So what?* he'd shouted back. *It doesn't mean you bloody own me.*

—You're not dying, Mam, he'd told her, in the hospital.

—Better to be prepared, anyway, she'd said. —We'll all be dying soon enough. Even Mr Do-It-All-On-His-Own here.

She'd smiled. She'd patted his hand.

—You're a great lad, she'd said. —I'm leaving it all to Anthony and the girls. There's a form he wants you to sign.

—Who?

—Seán Croft.

Croft was the lawyer. She'd been putting in the work.

—To stop any fuss that might happen after I go, she'd said. —Not that you'd ever make a fuss.

She'd smiled again.

—You understand.

No, I don't.

That was what he should have said. He should have taken the spoon from the yoghurt and smacked her on the forehead with it. He should have told her to name him, at least – leave him a ring or the microwave, just put his name back in the will. Let him exist. But he'd nodded. He understood. He was the adult, the independent one, the one who'd wanted nothing. And he'd understood, even then: she was killing him for it.

There was a smell now – an aroma – coming up from the pot. It would be heading out to the hall and up the stairs.

Jesus, though – he was tired.

He'd been drinking for days. He saw them now, the empties, through the back door glass. Lined up on the step. He could remember buying the first one. Going to the off-licence beside SuperValu – making that his daily walk. After he'd got the call from his brother.

—Mam died. Last night.

—Last night?

—Yeah.

—You're telling me now?

—I'm doing up a list of people who can attend the funeral. We're limited to ten.

—When's the funeral?

—I'll text you.

He knew he wouldn't be going. He couldn't believe it, but he knew. There'd be ten names ahead of him. His sisters, some grandkids, the surviving uncle.

—I'm making Anthony the executor, his mother had said. —I didn't think you'd mind. And he'll like it.

She'd laughed.

—He'll be the big boy.

And he'd laughed with her. He'd colluded. He'd killed himself.

He remembered drinking the first bottle. He remembered sitting in the kitchen. He remembered being hugged. He remembered outrage – Nell's, the kids'. None of his own.

—It's the lockdown – what else can he do?

He remembered falling over. Later. Onto the coffee table, in the front room, and onto the floor. Not being

126

able to get up. Alone. Cold. He remembered waking up beside Nell. He remembered surprise.

He won't be falling over again. He looked down at the dog, at his feet.

—That right, Jim?

He'd stay away from the car. He remembered now. Nell had taken the key – she'd hidden it. When he'd threatened to go to the church. He'd gone onto the street. He was going to smash the bottle he was carrying onto the lid of the coffin. He was going to pull off his mask and breathe all over the lucky ten – tell them all to fuck off and die. But he hadn't done any of that. He'd turned back – he'd staggered, but he'd turned and gone back inside.

He wasn't going to the graveyard. He wasn't going anywhere. He'd go back up to bed. *You were always the independent one*. He was going up to Nell, where he needed to be.

# Worms

He started to notice it one night, in the early days of the Corona. He was shaving – he always shaved at night – and that old song, 'The Whistling Gypsy', was there in his head. Not like a thought, but lower, at ear level, as if he was actually hearing the thing. He realised then, that particular night, that it wasn't the first time he'd heard the song while he shaved. And it happened again a few days later, the next time he was shaving. 'The Whistling Gypsy' was in his ears, both of them, although he could hear no real music.

It had been a big song when he was a kid. *Ah dee doo – ah dee doo da day*. His mother would have sung it in the kitchen and he was sure his father did too, or hummed it. But he couldn't remember either of them singing or whistling it. He had no idea why that song was in his head, or why it turned itself on only when he was shaving.

It was 'Back to My Roots' in the shower. He'd been out in the garden most of the day. He was feeling stiff and satisfied – none of the anxiety that had been in his shoulders for weeks – and 'Back to My Roots' was there, at his ears. Odyssey was the name of the band – in 1981 or '82. The song had never been a favourite

128

of his. But it was there when he bent down to pick up the soap. At that exact moment.

He was outside again the following afternoon, cutting the ivy back off the satellite dish – filling in the day, really. And when he was taking the lock off the shed door to go in and get the secateurs – the second he had the padlock in his hand – he started hearing 'Son of My Father', and he knew he'd heard the same thing the last time he'd held the lock. He opened a new page in the notes on his phone and he made a list of what he had so far – shaving, the shower, the padlock. He called the page Earworms, because he'd heard the term once and he'd liked it, a sound like a worm, wriggling, sliding, digging into your eardrum. He googled earworm – this was still out in the garden – and these songs he'd been hearing weren't earworms at all, strictly speaking. Because they weren't irritating or unwelcome. They only stayed a few seconds. They weren't songs he liked or disliked. 'Son of My Father' ended before the singing even started; it was just the opening part, the catchy synthesiser bit. 'Back to My Roots' was the first two lines and a *Yeah*. He looked at the list – the three titles, so far – and he began to see that his day might be full of these things. It didn't worry him. It was introspection. He supposed. He'd heard someone on the radio talking about introspection, a woman with a voice like an old-style air hostess. Introspection was only natural in these times, she'd said, and it wasn't something to be anxious about. 'We can do great things when we look within,' she'd said. She'd sounded too keen for the word. The radio had been full of over-keen voices. Working from home, walking with purpose, home-schooling, human capital – men and women screaming for a decent slice of the airtime. He'd thought that the introspective air hostess sounded a bit desperate. But not long after he'd heard her talk about the importance of making daily lists, he was making a list of his own.

He came in from the garden and he was pouring himself a mug of water. 'I'm Not in Love' – 'Big boys don't cry, big boys don't cry.' The second he put his hand on the cold tap. He added it to the list. He could feel it; he was really enjoying himself. And he was bending down, to see if it sparked off a song, when Thelma walked in and saw him.

—You're not in the right gear for ballet, Joseph, she said.

—Lay off.

—What are you doing?

The easiest thing was to show her the list.

—Oh, I love that one. Big boys don't cry.

The whole idea, it grabbed her.

—Come here, she said. —'Back to My Roots'. Does it start when the soap is in your hand?

—I don't know – I'm not sure. Why?

—Well, look it, she said. —The razor, the lock, the tap. The soap too, maybe. The songs arrive whenever you're holding something.

She took the breadknife off the counter and held it out for him. He took it. She stood back.

—Well?

—No.

—Nothing?

—Yeah – nothing.

—I might have contaminated it, she said.

He put the knife back down on the counter.

—It's all yours, he said.

—Open the fridge.

130

—No.

—Go on.

—Fuck off in a nice way, Thelma.

It was the longest conversation they'd had in weeks. It had been almost – Christ – flirtatious. And unsettling – it had definitely been unsettling. Joe felt like he was strolling into a trap.

The day after, she was showing him her own list.

—That one there, she said. —When I was leaning into the car.

Was she having a go at him? He looked at her, at the side of her face. There was nothing dangerous there, nothing getting ready to pounce. Her finger on the screen told him what to read.

—'It Don't Mean a Thing If It Ain't Got That Swing'.

—Twice, she said. —Putting the bags in – in the car park. I went across to Lidl. And I wanted to get away sharpish.

He was still looking at the song.

—I still had my mask on and that, she said. —And I didn't put the bags in the boot like normal. I opened the door behind my door and I was leaning in, to get the bags well in. And I heard 'It don't dah-dah-dah if it don't dah-dah-dah.' And then again – outside. Just now.

She left the phone with him and was emptying one of the shopping bags and spraying each item with the sanitiser they kept on the kitchen table.

—Do you get any songs when you're in or around the car, Joe?

—No.

—That's interesting.

—Why is it?

—Why me?

She was stealing his Lego – that was what it felt like. Pushing him away from the box. But she was smiling at him over her shoulder.


He heard 'Wichita Lineman' when he was out for his daily walk. Just the guitar solo, when he got to the top of the hill, when he could see the Dart station – the bridge – ahead of him.

He went home and told Thelma.

—Is there a hill in the song?

—What?

—When you got to the hill –.

—In the song?

—Yeah.

—No, he said. —The opposite.

—What's the opposite of a hill? she asked.

He remembered an interview with Glen Campbell, or it might have been Jimmy Webb, the guy who wrote the song. Webb or Campbell spoke about the flatness of the landscape. *You could stand on a matchbox and see for thirty miles.*

—Wichita, he said. —It's completely flat. That part of America.

He heard more worms but he kept them to himself. He divided them into categories and sub-categories. Touch, Mood, Favourites. Trying to make sense of them. He wondered if he was making a compilation of his life, an earworm autobiography. The razor was adult, the padlock was ownership. He didn't know what bending over in the shower was, but it made him laugh when he was looking at the list on the phone.

He was in the kitchen again. So was Thelma.

—A new one?

132

—No.

It was days since they'd had an earworm conversation. The last one had ended in a row. He suspected that Thelma had been cheating, coming up with song titles for the crack.

—Does anything ever happen when you're putting out the wheelies? she'd asked him.

—No, he said. —Why?

—Just – I heard 'Cracklin' Rosie', Thelma told him. —When I was out there.

—At the wheelie bins?

—Yeah.

—You never put the wheelies out, he said. —It's always me does that.

—That's why I was wondering.

—What?

—If it was one of yours, she said.

—'Cracklin' fuckin' Rosie'?

—It must be mine, so.

—You're a wagon, Thelma, he said.

—What?

—You're taking the piss.

—Ah, Joe. I'm not. It's just a bit of fun, though, isn't it?

He didn't answer. He was upset. He didn't know why, exactly. The list was a bit idiotic but, somehow, it was important. It was some sort of message to himself. A path, a map – he didn't know, he hadn't a clue. But he was interested in something – really interested – for the first time in years. And Thelma wasn't going to wreck it.

—Look, she said now, in the kitchen when she caught him laughing.

—What?

She was holding her phone in front of him. He could see it was open on Spotify.

—What am I looking at? he asked.

—My playlist, she said.

—Your what?

—All the songs, she said. —My worms. Different versions.

He took the phone off her and brought it up to his face.

—Did you know that Lonnie Donegan sang 'Kevin Barry'? she said.

—No, he said. —Did he?

—Imagine, she said. —The king of skiffle recording an Irish rebel song.

He'd had no idea that she knew what skiffle was. He hadn't known that she had Spotify.

—Will we do it together? she said.

—What?

—Compile the songs, she said.

She looked straight at him. And he looked straight back. For the first time in years. He realised that as he did it.

—Okay, he said.


They spent hours listening to the worms and covers of the worms.

—See, that's a big difference between us, she said.

—What? he said. —Go on.

He'd fallen in love with his wife.

—I'll tell you, she said. —You call them covers and I just call them versions.

—The songs – you're talkin' about the songs?

—Yeah.

—Is that all? he said.

—You think they're precious and I think they're only oul' songs.

She laughed.

He could feel it – he *knew* it. She understood him. She got him. Thirty-four years after they'd met. And he got her – he thought. He hoped. Something had happened. They'd opened up to each other. He wasn't sure why – it made no real sense.

—It was your face, she told him.

—What about my face?

—I could see into you, she said.

—Sorry, he said. —What do you mean?

—When you were talking about your worms, she said. —Or thinking about them. Your guard was down. I could see who you were.

—Really?

—And I liked you, she said.

She smiled.

—And what about me? she said.

—What about you?

—Some things don't change, it seems.

—You're different, he said.

—Am I?

—No, he said. —That's not it. I don't mean you're different. I mean – there's more of you.

—Ah, here –.

—More *to* you. There's more to you – that's what I mean.

—That feels a bit – well – well, a bit hurtful.

—I know, he said. —And I want to apologise.

—Okay, she said. —For what, though?

They were in the bed. Neither of them had moved.

—For not – like –. For not getting to know you properly. I think.

—Grand.

—And I really like you.

—What are we like?

—I don't know, he said.

—I was being –. I think I was being facetious.

—I know, he said. —But it's true. I don't know what we're like.

—'The Whistling Gypsy' has to go, she said.

—What?

—I can't find an even half-decent version, she said.

—So what? said Joe. —It's what I hear when I'm shaving.

—Well, it's not going on the playlist.

—What's your problem, Thelma?

It wasn't a minefield any more. It was pleasure.

—D'you know who sang that song, Joe? she said.

—Who?

—Barney.

—The dinosaur?

—The purple fucking dinosaur.

—He's not the only one, surely.

—Well, she said. —I thought –. I thought Nick Cave or someone was bound to have done it. Even once – at a gig. For a laugh. Or Tom Waits. Or Willie Nelson.

—Kate Bush.

—Perfect, she said. —But even someone uncool would do. Just human.

—John Denver.

—Crystal Gayle – or Leo Sayer.

It wasn't that she'd taken a sudden interest in music, or the music he was into. It was years since he, himself, had been into anything. Not just the modern stuff. He knew that Taylor Swift and Stormzy existed but he'd no idea what they sounded like. The music he'd grown

136

up with, the albums that he'd thought defined him – he'd stopped listening to them, years ago. But then, in the pandemic, in what became the first lockdown, he was back listening to music. But it was better this time; it was fun. The worms weren't the bigots that he'd been when he was nineteen. He was happy enough listening to anything.

—It's called 'The Happy Wanderer' as well, said Thelma.

—What is?

—'The Whistling Gypsy', she said. —They're the same song – listen.

They shared her headphones, a bud each, like teenage girls, their heads resting against each other. They listened to a version of 'The Happy Wanderer' that had been in *The Sopranos*, sung by Frankie Yankovic. Joe had never felt more at home, or excited. Leaning against this woman who he'd discovered he'd been married to for more than thirty years.

—That's not the same song, he said.

He was delighted – he didn't know why. And so was she.

—Is it not?

—No, he said. —They're completely different.

He didn't pull the bud from his ear. She didn't pause the song.

—That's a relief, she said. —It's dreadful. What's 'The Wandering Gypsy' then?

—It's not *foller-ee-foller-ah*, he said. —It's *ah dee doo, ah dee doo da day*.

He watched her fingers travelling across her phone. Her sixty-year-old fingers. He wanted to bend and kiss the knuckles. But he didn't want to interrupt her. He wanted to watch as she searched for the song.

—Ah, she said. —Here. Yet another name – 'The Gypsy Rover'. The Clancy Brothers sang it. Here we go – brace yourself, Joseph.

Was this the new life? The third age someone had tried to tell him about? He couldn't remember who – it was so long since he'd stood in front of anyone and chatted. He thought it was one of the men he knew in the pub who'd been yapping on about the third age, like an estate agent trying to sell it. He hadn't really listened. Your life was your life, he'd thought. You took what came at you.

But he wondered. He'd been miserable – for years, before the lockdown. He got up, made it through the day, went to bed, got up. The lockdown hadn't made much difference – until he met Thelma. Re-met her. They were laughing together one day and they'd looked at each other and he'd started to cry, and so had she. He'd gone to hug her. She'd let him.

—I'm sorry, he said.

She knew what he meant.

—Me too, she said. —Will we get a takeaway? To celebrate.

She sighed the night when they heard that the travel restrictions were being lifted. They were sitting together, watching the News. There was a chart on the screen, the various categories of workers and when they could start going back to work.

—It's good, I suppose.

—Ah, it is.

They stopped watching the News. They stayed in their lockdown. They shopped just twice a week. They stayed clear of the brothers and sisters, the cousins and friends. They said no to all the picnics and barbeques. They used Thelma's asthma. She had to be careful,

138

they said. And they were left alone. The word was out; Thelma had an underlying condition. The asthma hadn't been a thing in Thelma's life in years, decades – since, Joe estimated, a couple of years after they got married. There'd been a line they'd had back then – *Is that passion or asthma?* – one of a string of gags they'd made their own until the asthma seemed to just go, quietly, and the jokes and bits of phrases went with it.

—D'you remember the Ventolin orgasm? Joe asked her one day, after she got off the phone with her sister.

—We were hilarious, she said.

—What actually happened your asthma? he asked her.

—Well, she said. —I was always told that I'd probably grow out of it. And that's what happened – I suppose. Giving birth is my bet.

They had a new rule that they both loved: they weren't allowed to talk about the kids. They had a room upstairs, the boys' old bedroom, where they went if they had anything to say about the children, or if they were going to phone or Zoom them. The panic room, they called it.

Thelma referring to the birth of their eldest, in the sitting room – it took seconds for Joe to catch up.

—You never said anything at the time, he said. —I don't think you did.

—I probably didn't notice, she said. —But some sort of a psychological shift – that'd be my theory. Today.

—Amazing, really – isn't it?

—I suppose it is, she said.

What neither of them said was that, really – they'd stopped talking. The words they'd spoken to each other, and there were a lot of them – millions – were exchanges of information as they passed each other in the kitchen,

139

on the stairs, as one of them got out of the car and the other got in, as they got into bed and out of bed. And that habit, that practice, that polite desolation, had continued long after the kids were gone. Until the worms slid into his life, and her life. Into their lives. Their life.

—Well, it's back, Joe said. —Officially. Your asthma.

—In name only.

—Do you feel guilty? he asked.

—Not a bit.

They got through the summer, the autumn and into the second lockdown without too much interference. The kids came to visit, one at a time. They weren't invited to stay.

—Can I use the washing machine?

—No – sorry.

—Why not?

—Because you'll have to come back to collect it. That's not on. And you can't stay overnight.

—That's ridiculous.

—Your mother's been advised, love. We've to limit the visits. Because of her asthma.

—She doesn't have asthma.

—I do.

—You never had asthma when we were small, like.

—That's because I was too busy with yours.

—I didn't have asthma – that was Colm.

—I wasn't being literal, sweetheart. But the asthma's real – sorry. And so is the Covid. It'll be different at Christmas – won't it, Joe?

—Yeah, said Joe. —Open house.

They watched Micheál Martin on the News announcing the careful opening up of the country. The phrase he used – a meaningful Christmas – felt more insidious than any virus. But they knew they'd have to let the family in. They remembered their first Christmas together, when Thelma had been pregnant and they'd told the others – her family, his family – that they'd be spending it alone, just the two of them. There'd been war and they'd called the house Stalingrad for a while – another joke they'd forgotten – but they'd won. They'd had the day they'd wanted – a ride, a chicken, a pile of rented videos.

—We could do it again, said Joe. —Could we?

—No, said Thelma.

—Okay.

—I kind of miss them.

—Me too – I think.

—Grand.

She sighed, and smiled.

—Wait and see, she said. —The whole country will go mad and there'll have to be another lockdown straight after.

—Maybe.

—Definitely.

They went to one of her sister's, and then on to one of his. They didn't hug anyone, and they didn't stay anywhere for too long; they walked in wearing their masks. Two of the kids came to the house for a couple of days. They endured it all cheerfully. The pubs and restaurants would be shutting again on Christmas Eve and the home visits would be stopped. They put the turkey on the table knowing that they were almost into the third lockdown.

But it was different.

*

Joe woke and knew, immediately: they were in trouble. Thelma wasn't awake but she was whimpering. She was in a fight against something he couldn't see. He put a hand on her shoulder and felt the heat. His hold seemed to calm her. The whimpering died but a wheeze, a gentle rattle, had replaced it.

—Okay?

She was lying on her back now, still asleep.

—Thelma?

Something was happening – he had to be ready. He went down to the kitchen and found the box where they kept the old medicines and plasters. He rooted through the empty packets and foil blister packs. He was hoping he'd see the strange blue of a Ventolin inhaler. Or the other one, the brown one – Becotide. He didn't know what good either of them would do but he remembered the blue one in Thelma's fist – years ago. He remembered her shaking it, bringing it quickly to her mouth, the gasp when she pressed the silver top with her thumb – actually, the bottom – and the seconds, the eternity, until she took the thing away from her mouth. He knew as he searched: there wasn't an inhaler in the house. But there was a song in his fuckin' ear.

She was still asleep when he got back to the bedroom with a glass of water in case she wanted it. He brought a chair in from the panic room and sat at the window. He googled asthma and Covid but he couldn't read; the words weren't sticking. He threw his phone on the bed.

He must have drifted. His neck was sore when he became aware that she was turning in the bed. He heard her gasp.

—Thelma – love?

He stood so he could see her properly. Her eyes were open; she was staring at something that wasn't in the room.

—Okay?

He saw a slight nod – he thought he did.

—A bad dream?

There was no nod this time, no shake of the head. He leaned in, put his hand across her forehead. She was hot, and wet. She lifted her hand and gripped his wrist. She was holding on to him; he could feel that. Her hand was clammy – and, somehow, not hers.

—I heard another one, he told her. —Downstairs.

She squeezed his wrist.

—'The Hustle', he said.

He thought he saw her smile.

—Man-on-a-mission music, he said.

—No man I'd want – to know, she said.

She was fine – he'd just heard the proof. He grabbed his phone off the bed.

—Will I play it?

—No, she said.

She gasped. She whimpered.

—I'll phone the doctor.

She didn't answer.

She came downstairs. He stayed in the kitchen, so she wouldn't see him watching her. She came in and took her bag off the table.

—I'll come with you, he said.

—No, she said.

She looked okay. She sounded okay.

—Better for you to stay here, she said.

—If you have it, I have it, he said.

—No, she said.

He showed her the Croke Park testing centre on his phone, and the route from where they were standing.

—It's not the usual way you'd go if you were going to Croke Park, he told her.

—I've never been to Croke Park, she said.

—Just look at the map, he said. —Stop being fuckin' cranky.

—Yes, master.

She stood beside him.

—Are you sure about this?

—Has to be done, she said.

He followed her out to the car.

—Are you sure? he said.

—Go back inside, Joe, she said.

She kept him fed through the day with a stream of texts. *The Q – FFS!* He replied, but asked no questions. She was home by the end of the afternoon. She'd texted him when she was leaving Croke Park, on her way home. And he could check his calls and confirm that he'd phoned for the ambulance after he'd phoned the GP. There were two days, almost exactly forty-eight hours, between her text and his second phone call. She'd come home – he knew she had. But when he was asked to account for the two days – when he asked himself what had happened – all he could say was, It got worse.

He remembered bringing her water. He remembered telling her that 'These Boots are Made for Walking' had slid into his ear on his way up the stairs. He remembered waiting for her to say something. He remembered feeling like a fool for mentioning it, especially as it wasn't true. He'd heard nothing, just her struggling to breathe before he got to the bedroom door.

The television was on when the ambulance lads brought Thelma down the stairs. It was right behind him – he hadn't been watching it. He fought the urge to go in and turn it off while he stood at the sitting room door and watched them – and Thelma – pass, and go out. He stood outside and checked that he had his keys in his pocket in case he locked himself out, and he watched as one of the men shut the back door of the ambulance and climbed into the front. He didn't look at Joe. Joe stayed there, halfway between the door and the gate, until the ambulance had gone around the corner. He went back in. He turned off the television, then turned it back on. She'd been gone five minutes but it felt like days – or longer. He tried to remember when they'd last spoken properly. He couldn't hear her voice.

He slept where he sat.

He phoned the children. He must have – they phoned him back. They left food outside the door. They texted him. They sent him the names of forensic dramas that they knew he'd like. They WhatsApped him a video of Guards dancing – cops all over the country dancing to a catchy tune in front of perfect scenery. He looked at it for hours, again and again, and cried.


The phone rang on the couch beside him. It was a Dublin number, not a name. He looked at it, then picked it up.

—Hello?

—Hello there – am I talking to Joe?

—Yes.

—Hi, Joe – I'm calling from St Joseph's ward –.

—Oh –.

—No – it's fine – no. Joe – do you have an iPad or a tablet? Aoife wasn't sure.

—Aoife?

—Your daughter.

—Christ – yeah. Sorry – yeah.

He laughed.

—Sorry.

—No, no –. Do you?

He had to think.

—Yes, he said.

—Grand.

She was going to call him again in the morning, at ten – the girl; if she'd told him her name he'd forgotten it. He was going to answer on the iPad and he'd see Thelma – he'd be able to see Thelma.

—Will she be awake? he asked.

—Hopefully she will.

—Yeah. Thank you.

He looked at himself in the bathroom mirror. It was days since he'd shaved and he wanted to look normal for Thelma in the morning. He was drying his face when he realised that he hadn't heard 'The Whistling Gypsy'.


It was hard to know her on the screen. He'd expected the oxygen and the tubes. He'd seen enough hospital wards on the News over the past year, and nurses and doctors in the bee-keeper gear – he didn't let himself be shocked.

—Here she is, said the nurse holding the iPad – her name was Úna.

—Do you see who's here, Thelma? she said.

He wanted to tell her to shut up. He just wanted to look at Thelma. He wanted to recognise her.

146

—Is she awake?

—She is.

He couldn't see that. The screen was too close to her. Her skin didn't look like skin. Her face wasn't hers. Her hair was pushed way back off her head.

—Howyeh, Thelma, he said.

—Hear that now, Thelma? It's Joe – isn't it?

—Are they feeding you properly, Thelma?

He wanted it to end.

—Oh, we are. But maybe not up to your usual standard, if I'm being honest. Am I right, Thelma?

There was no movement. The shape he was looking at – it didn't shift or react. The sounds came from under liquid. He was shaking when it was over and already dreaded having to do it again.

There was no change the next day. She looked the same.

He didn't ask questions. The kids did, and they told him the answers.

—Will she be coming out? That's all I want to know.

It was a horrible thing to ask, forcing the answer from one of his children.

—Don't – sorry. You're doing your best. I understand. I just miss her.

—So do I, Dad.

—I know, love.

Every morning, for ten days – his slot was ten o'clock – he sat at the kitchen table and waited for the call. He held up the iPad with one hand and pressed the green circle.

The screen this time, the camera – he was looking straight at her face. The mask was off, beside her on the pillow, leaning against her ear.

She was saying something – speaking.

—I – heard – one. Joe.

—Did you? he said.

He seemed to see each word before he heard it.

—At first – I was – afraid – I was pet – rified.

He knew the song.

—'I Will Survive', he said.

The words were heavy – she worked hard at pulling them out.

—I – might.

—Jesus – I love you, he said.

Something struck him now, the thought that had been lurking for months.

—Your worms, he said. —You've been making them up all the time, haven't you?

He looked at her mouth on the screen, and waited. It was ages before she answered.

# The Five Lamps

He saw Dublin on the News – the streets empty, no one at all on them. And he thought to himself, I'll find him now. So he went there, straight to Dublin. He filled the car – a sleeping bag, a duvet, the jacket, some extra clothes, the phone charger, a couple of bottles of water. Things he thought of, without thinking too much. There was no dog to feed, no one or nothing else to consider. He just went.

You weren't allowed to go anywhere – that was the thing. He didn't know what he'd say if he was stopped – he didn't overthink it. If the Guards stopped him and sent him back, he'd turn for home and he'd turn again at the first left he came to. He'd make it to the edge of Dublin and walk the rest of the way if he had to. He was going to find the boy. The Covid had cleared the path for him. It would be now or maybe never.

It was only the second day of the lockdown. There wasn't a thing on the road. It was night – it was two in the morning. The rear-view was black, there was nothing behind him. He was on a straight stretch of the motorway – he knew it well. There wasn't a tail light ahead, for miles. He stayed away from the radio. He was the only man in the world.

There were no checkpoints in his way. He got on to the M50 and stayed on it. He decided to gamble, around the city instead of straight in. He'd go in like a spacecraft coming back through the atmosphere. He'd enter the city sideways.

He knew Dublin. The map in his head wasn't out of date. He came and he went on a fairly regular basis. There was a place where he'd had a flat years ago. He parked in the public car park in front of the sea. There was one other car, no one sitting in it, at the other end of the tarmac. The road behind him, into town, was bare of cars and buses. He put the car under a lamp and waited till daylight. There wasn't a rush hour. The road into the city stayed empty.

He ate a banana. He took a mouthful of water, grabbed his jacket from behind him, and got out of the car. He'd walk into the city from here. That way – that approach – he'd have more to see; he'd cross more streets, stop at more corners. In the dreams he always walked; he never saw the boy from a moving window.

It wasn't cold – it wasn't too bad. From where he stood he could look at the bay and the Irish Sea behind it, at the mountains beyond the docks, at the city itself – Liberty Hall, the Spire. He could see the weather clear from three directions. There were no surprises coming his way. He was stiff from the driving and thinking. He wondered when the stiffness had started, when he'd begun to live with it. He didn't know.

He got going.

Under the old railway bridge, past a big gym that hadn't been there back in his Dublin days; along the side of Fairview Park. He'd played football there the odd time, with other lads from the flats and bedsits around. He passed the pub, Gaffney's. Croke Park wasn't far off – he remembered. Edge's Hardware. Past a fire station he'd no memory of. This was the city, he thought – he felt – as he started walking up the hill to the bridge over the canal. He was in Dublin now, proper. The stiffness was out of him. This was where he'd find the boy.

And what would he do then?

He had it in his head, what the boy would be like. He'd had the picture now for a long time. He'd have the beard he'd been starting when he left. He'd have one of the caps all the young lads wore. A tattoo, on his neck, more than likely. He'd say nothing about it when he found him; he wouldn't gawk at it. There'd be another tattoo, on one of his hands, maybe. A swallow. Between the thumb and index finger. His left hand – he was left-handed. He'd be taller than him by now. His mother had been a tall woman. He'd be a man. But the boy would still be in him. The eyes – *her* eyes – would still be looking out at him, from under the hair.

—There's just me and you now, son.

—Why?

—We'll be grand.

—Where's Mam after going?

—God knows.

—Fuck God.

—You're not to be saying that.

—What has fuckin' God got to do with this? Don't be blaming fuckin' God.

—Don't be talking like that.

—Where's she gone?

★

151

Maybe two cars had gone by him in the half-hour. And an empty bus. And not a sinner on the footpaths, no one, until he came up to the Five Lamps. He was looking properly now. This was where he'd see the boy. At a corner, or sitting on a step. In the dreams he'd less control over, the boy would be scurrying, in a corner of his eye, down an alley, through the bricks – gone. This was the inner city now, here. Dangerous and deprived, unpredictable, notorious. Where the heroin was, where the shootings happened. Where the famous Dublin wit came from. The heart of real Dublin – he'd never known it, really. He'd only looked at it from the bus or, now and again, a taxi window. It had changed a bit since his own Dublin days. The office block on the corner to his left looked wet it was so new, like something pasted to cardboard. But the Five Lamps were still there, on the island where five streets met, the North Strand, Portland Row, Amiens Street, Seville Place – he couldn't remember the name of the fifth street. The big black base with the lions' heads on its sides, and the lamps themselves, one at the top and the other four on separate arms. They'd been there long enough to have had bodies hanging from them, he thought, back in the days of pikes and barefoot urchins, dead bodies swinging in the wind.

This – here – was where the boy was. Somewhere around here. He had a photograph on his phone. It was four years old. He shut his eyes – they shut themselves – when he thought of that. Four years since he took the picture. More than four. He was looking straight into the camera, holding up a chip, grinning in that half way of his. The pair of them had been out mending a fence most of the day, the fingers frozen off them. He'd never forget the guffaw out of the boy when he leaned on a post they'd just hammered into place and it toppled over before he'd his elbow properly resting on it. The chips and a zombie film – they were the reward for what the boy had called a job done shite. There had been good times, good days.

This was the start of Dublin's central business district. The CBD. He remembered it from geography – one of the few things he remembered, even though he'd done geography for three years in UCD, and he'd even taught it for a year. He remembered the lecture about the CBD. He could even remember where he'd put himself sitting in the lecture hall, and the girl he'd liked sitting with her pal two rows below, a bit to his left so he could see her profile when she was writing her notes. He couldn't remember her name; it was possible he'd never known it. And he couldn't remember the lecturer's name. He was one of the younger ones, jeans and a waistcoat over his black T-shirt. He switched on the overhead projector and slapped the transparency onto the glass, and there it was, the definition. He wrote it down while he watched the girl do the same – 'The Central Business District is the commercial and business center of a city.' He remembered it now for two reasons. One was the spelling of 'center'. Your man, the lecturer, must have lifted the definition out of an American textbook. It was the first time he'd seen that spelling and he'd thought it was a mistake – and he'd loved that, the fact that the lecturer spelt a word wrong. The other reason came later, when he was on his way back home to the flat. He was looking out the bus window, passing the Five Lamps, where he was stood now, and he'd concluded that Dublin didn't have a proper central business district. He hated the place. He'd always hated the place.

He saw a skinny young lad in a black hoodie. He was heading up Portland Row, up to where Croke Park was. He thought about following him. If he'd been in a film he'd definitely have gone after him. The lad would have been leading him to something significant. But it wasn't a film. He kept going straight, along Amiens Street. He could have walked down the middle of it, it was so empty. He walked past a line, a terrace, of buildings held up by rusted iron props, the whole side of the street waiting to be demolished. There was only the facade, he reckoned, nothing behind it. He'd thought of the boy climbing in behind there, somewhere like that, at night, with a damp sleeping bag or a blanket, looking for a place to lie down. Often, he'd done it – pictured it. He'd had to stop the car once, he'd had to get out and walk around, to turn the certainty back into a notion, only a picture in his head.

There were men sitting on steps in front of one of the Georgian doors Dublin was famous for, across the street. And others standing around – seven people he counted. Five men, two women – and a buggy, a baby or a toddler in it. It was exactly the kind of place where he'd pictured himself finding the boy. But not like this, not with other men. He could feel a knot, the hard, tight end of a rope, low down in his gut, pulling at him, trying to stop him. He had to pull against it, against himself. He waited till he was right opposite the steps and the door. A rough-looking gang they were, none of them standing still or sitting still. Shouting at one another. He didn't need to read the sign beside the door. It was a methadone clinic – he could tell. They were waiting. It was early, still. They were terrified, probably, that the door wasn't going to open for them.

This was what frightened him. This was what he hated. He'd cross, and one of the men would turn and be his boy.

He stepped onto the street. There was no traffic – he didn't have to look. But you forgot how wide a city street could be. It felt like he was in one of those dreams he had. Moving but making no progress, in a half-demolished landscape. Looking for something – he didn't know what, till he woke up and knew. And this, now, wasn't a dream. It was Dublin on Day Three of the lockdown. The pain in his gut was digging down into him; he needed to go for a piss. That was something he'd forgotten about, how he'd manage it, with everywhere shut. He kept walking and got to the other side. He was hoping he looked like he owned his share of the footpath.

One of the men was looking his way. A boy, until you saw him properly. The face was well past boyhood – a middle-aged man stuck in a kid's stance.

—Are you new, are yeh?

He was taken aback, already caught out.

—What d'you mean?

—Are you goin' in? D'yeh work in there?

—No.

Some of the others were looking at him now.

He spoke to the woman with the buggy. He could see there were teeth gone but there was something beautiful still clinging to her.

—I'm looking for my son, he said.

—Are yeh?

—Yes.

—What's his name, love?

He told her – them.

—Don't know him, I don't think.

The others, the ones who were interested, didn't know the name.

—Does he have a nickname, love – somethin' else?

—I don't know.

He took out his phone – he decided to do it. He showed her the photo. She reached out to hold the phone, but stopped.

—Better not, she said. —The Corona.

She looked at the picture of the boy. She smiled.

—Ah, look it.

The others looked.

—Where d'yeh get the fuckin' chips, man? The chippers are all shut.

—Give us a look – here.

She stood between the other men and him.

—He's a dote, he is, she said.

She shook her head.

—I don't know him, but.

She nodded at the phone.

—How old is the picture, love?

He didn't hesitate.

—Four years, he said.

—God, she said. —Are yeh sure he's here – in Dublin, like?

—I think so.

—We'll keep an eye out, said the man who'd first spoken to him. —Give us your number there.

He put the phone back in his pocket and stepped off the path.

—Thank you, he said.

He crossed the street. He half-expected them, or some of them, to follow. They'd be on him, all over him, in his pockets. Stupid, he realised. They were waiting for the clinic to open; there were other priorities. He looked back, just glanced. None of them were watching him. This was where the gangland killings were, though. The place was a drugs supermarket – he'd heard a local, a Dub, say that on the radio. It wasn't safe at any time of the day.

He stuck to his plan. He turned on to Talbot Street. He stopped at the top, beside the memorial, the stone slab with the names on it, the people who'd died in the 1974 bombing. The list of names on the stone – it was powerful. He read them, and knew he was looking for the boy's name. It was mad, he knew, but that didn't stop him. He looked the length of the street, to the Spire in the distance. He saw no one. There were lanes – alleys around here. There'd be a wall he could piss against. He'd risk the CCTV cameras.

He found a wall. Shame and relief seeped up through him as he let go, and he got back quickly on to Talbot Street. He wouldn't be washing his hands this time. He hadn't washed his hands since he'd left home. There were things he hadn't thought through. He'd get sanitiser somewhere, and wipes.

Talbot Street – this was Dublin's CBD. It was empty, the shithole it had always been. Grafton Street had a bit going for it; you could persuade yourself you were in London or even Paris if you wore blinkers and blocked your ears. But this place – danger at every corner, seagulls in charge of the air, half the premises already shut down, just waiting for the pandemic to put them out of their misery – this was Dublin. There wasn't one thing about this street that summoned a fondness. He stood on the corner of Gardiner Street. To the right the railings and steps, the Georgian decay where he'd pictured the boy. Left – the river that stank in the summers when he was a young man. He'd seen the boy there too in his mind, on a bench on the boardwalk, always with his cheekiness intact, sitting up on the back of the bench and his feet on the seat, looking straight back at the world as it passed.

—You know fuckin' nothing about me.
    —I do. What don't I know?
    —What subjects do I do – in school, like? I go to school during the day.
    —Sometimes – you do.
    —Name them – go on. Name fuckin' one of them.
    —English, Maths –.
    —The options – come on. You haven't a clue.
    —French –.
    —You don't know and you don't care.
    —Do you do French – tell us?
    —That's why Mam left.
    —And she was better, was she? And she's coming back for you, is she?

There were people on O'Connell Street. There'd always be people on O'Connell Street. Even after the end of the world there'd be some maggot walking down O'Connell Street. There were four or five of them on the street, up where the Carlton used to be and down nearer the river. They moved in that jagged, restless way of the addicts. They were the grandchildren of the junkies who'd frightened him when he was a young lad, when drugs had been a problem unique to Dublin – and deserved, he'd sometimes thought, before he'd left. Hoods up, hidden yet brazen – there was no point in trying to catch up with them. None of them was the

158

boy. Scum, he'd thought back then. Dublin scum. Or the word he'd heard a lot in the school, in the yard and on the corridors: scumbags.

He'd go left, to the river.

The clock over Eason's said twenty to ten. In his bones, it felt much later. His feet – his legs – were already sore. The sweat was cooling on him; he was going to be cold for the rest of the day. He was hungry. He hadn't thought the thing through at all. But he had – he'd thought about it for years. He was going to find the boy; that was all the thinking he needed. This Coronavirus coming into the country was the impetus he'd wanted, the signal. It wasn't hunger in him; it was urgency. When he'd seen the width of O'Connell Street, empty, on the television – exactly where he was standing now – he'd stood up and started bringing things he'd be needing to the car. Something about the image, the openness of it, nothing moving or hidden – it was the message he'd been waiting for.

He walked along the river, to Heuston Station. On a bench on the boardwalk, early on, as he came up to the Ha'penny Bridge, he saw a couple of men, grown men in sturdy looking jackets, sitting still, staring at the water. He'd take out the phone, he decided. He could show these lads the picture. They were men like himself – until he was up close, the safe two metres, and he thought for a second that the men were both dead. There was a bag of cans and bottles between them on the bench and they were drunk, solid drunk – literally ossified. They were Polish looking – builders, maybe, big boots on them, with nowhere to go and the sites all shut. They'd been sitting like that for hours, days. It scared him more than the junkies. He could imagine himself like that. It was more than two years since he'd had a drink but he'd been well able to drink himself shut. He could feel it as he walked on; he could feel its appeal.

There was normally a homeless lad or two sitting on the Ha'penny Bridge, and dozens of visitors doing the selfies. But the bridge was empty and there was no one across on the steps, at the archway into Temple Bar. It looked like a big hole into nothing. The nearer he got to the station, the more it seemed like he was the only man living. He saw someone – he thought it was a woman – crossing the street, up at Christ Church. But she was too far away, too distant to be young or old, and Christ Church looked small and nothing special without the traffic going past and under it. There were corners further up the river, blocks knocked or never built, or badly built – the landscape of the dreams he had when he was searching for the boy.

A Luas tram came out from the street that ran beside Collins Barracks. It crossed the quay in front of him, as he came up to the station. There was nobody on it, it looked like – absolutely no one. He didn't even see the driver. He walked into the station, and through it. There was a train drawing away, from the Cork platform. There were a couple of people with cases. He looked at the list of destinations and the train times. It wasn't doing the usual flickering. There wasn't one place up there that he'd have wanted to go to, including the town he'd driven from the night before. Only the night before – it felt like a different life. He walked around the pillars and went outside, where the taxis lined up.

There was a girl once; he met her in a pub the year he was teaching. A Dublin young one – he'd been surprised when she'd spoken to him, when she'd come back with him to the flat, when she'd come back again, and again, when she'd phoned the school staffroom to see what he was up to. She was lying beside him one night. She'd leaned out off the bed and turned on the radio. He'd held her so she didn't slide to the floor. She'd laughed as she pushed herself back up onto the bed. 'Midnight Train to Georgia' – that was the song they heard as she lay down and put her head on his chest.

—That's you, isn't it?

—What?

—On the midnight train to Mullingar.

—I'm not from Mullingar, he said.

—Yeah.

He couldn't see her face, just her hair, the top of her head.

She sang.

—Duh-blin – it proved too much for the man.

—There's nothing fuckin' special about Dublin, he said.

She patted his stomach.

—Then why d'yis keep comin' here? she said. —I'm only slaggin' you.

She lifted her head, pushed her hair back off her face, and smiled.

It was Dublin all over, he'd decided, after they'd stopped seeing each other. They thought the rest of the world was unlucky. Even the junkies were proud of the place.

He'd thought of her since. Often, he'd thought of her. He'd wondered if he'd know her if they met, bumped into each other. Here, even. The same age as him.

—Is it you? she'd say. —Jesus.

She'd be looking well. She'd smile. She'd remember.

—Still waitin' for the midnight train.

He often remembered her head on his chest, his hand on her hair. He'd made up a story for himself. She'd found the boy; she'd been looking after him. They were waiting for him. It was madness, just stupid. The boy had been born ten years after he'd last seen that girl. His mother was a different woman. But, still, he'd let himself tell it and add to it, when it was raining bad out or there was a murder – a stabbing or a shooting – on the News. The boy was with the Dublin girl – the woman. She'd seen him on the street and she'd seen something in him – she'd known he was his dad.

He was an eejit. Trying to rub out his life.

He'd tell the boy that when he found him. And he'd tell him other things.

He bought a sandwich in a plastic-and-cardboard box, and a bottle of water, at a kiosk in the station. He was the only customer. He held out a tenner to the girl. She looked at it in his hand.

—You have card?

—Why?

He looked at his hand, and at the note shaking slightly.

—My boss tells not to handle cash, said the girl.

He only really noticed her mask now. He'd been looking at the anxiety in her eyes, wondering why his outstretched hand was causing it.

—Right, he said. —I wasn't thinking.

He dug inside his jacket for his wallet.

—Everyone is same, like.

—I just tap, yeah?

—Yes – that is right.

—It's quiet enough.

—Yes, she said. —You want receipt?

—No – thanks.

He remembered the photo. This was someone he could show it to, the same age as the boy.

He held the screen in front of her.

—Have you seen this lad?

He expected her to nod. He really did. There was something about her – she wanted to.

—No, she said. —I do not think so.

—He'd be a bit older now, he said. —My son he is.

—He is missing?

—I don't know, he said. —I mean – I haven't seen him. In a bit.

—Send me photograph, she said.

She was getting her phone from beside the till.

—If I see him I will message.

—You'll send me a text?

—Yes.

—Are you serious?

She hesitated. He could see her translating what he'd said.

—Yes, she said.

She slowly called out her number – he imagined she'd gone at this pace before, for her parents and grandparents – while he tapped the digits into his phone. She told him her name, so he could put that in too. He held the phone over the counter while she taught him how to send the photograph.

He heard her phone.

—You got it there?

She looked.

—Yes.

—Great, he said. —Look – thank you.

—It is nothing.

—Ah, it is. It means the world.

★

163

The bread was damp and tasteless but he was still tempted to turn back to the station and buy another from the girl. But he knew it would worry her, even scare her, him coming back so soon. He'd have hated to see that happening in front of him. He kept walking, back down to the city centre, along the other bank of the river. There was no sign of life, except the occasional car and lorry, the odd distant figure. He passed no one, no one passed him. The Guinness place looked deserted, like it had been locked up years before. He thought about turning uphill, onto one of the streets off the quays and the streets off them. But he'd stay close to the river, he decided. He'd do it differently if he was still searching the next day. In his head, the way he'd seen it rolling, he found the boy quickly. The decision had been the thing, and the timing. The rest of it was effortless. He looked out for the names of the bridges as he walked past them – he hadn't known most of them before. Sherwin, Rory O'More, James Joyce, Mellows, Father Matthew. Priests, rebels, writers – all the clichés. He kept waiting for something – he didn't know what, exactly – something, a vista, to open before him at each bridge and corner. There'd be more to see, a new angle. He'd take a few more steps, into the wider space, and the boy would be there.

But he wasn't there.

He *was* there, just hidden, waiting to be found. He'd always been a passive kind of lad – until he'd left.

He checked the time on his phone. It wasn't even midday.


He was lucky with the weather. He was able to sit in the car with the door open. Or he could sit in one of the shelters along the promenade. He could sit on the sea wall. But he was nervous about sitting for too long. He thought he might seize up. He didn't know how far he'd walked – how many kilometres it was to Heuston Station and back to the car. He wasn't tired, though, not at all. But sore, with the disappointment. It was in the body, at his joints, and a big hand pushing down on his head. Buses had passed as he'd walked back to the car. But he didn't want to get on a bus. He never saw the boy from a window. He was always on foot. The finding, the seeing of the boy, was easy. It was getting to the spot, the point where he'd see him. That was the labour. The day had taught him that. It was a pilgrimage he was on. He'd have to be sore and he'd have to be thirsty. Shortcuts weren't going to work. He'd have to walk through the disappointment, the pessimism, his own voice at him to go on home. He'd walk in his bare feet if he had to. He'd throw his boots in the sea after the third day, if he hadn't found the boy by then – he was serious. He'd take the punishment.

He had the radio on in the car; he left the engine idling, to keep it alive and to charge his phone. There was a man going on about washing the hands, the importance of it. Sing 'Happy Birthday', he was saying. He wouldn't be washing his hands. Every tap in Dublin was behind a locked door. If he used bottled water the bottle would be empty before he got to the first *You*, even one of the big bottles. He'd gone into the Spar at the Five Lamps. He'd bought biscuits and wipes, and a plastic yoke of chopped fruit, mostly apple. And toilet paper.

The news on the radio was all numbers. Deaths in Lombardy, hospital admissions in the Republic and the

North. He had the car facing the water. The path was in front of him too. He watched the way people moved, avoiding one another. He couldn't see feet; it was like they were all on skis – swerving. And not many people. The car park was almost empty. You weren't supposed to go further than two kilometres from your home. He knew – sitting in his car, with its Longford reg – he was drawing attention to himself. He was breaking the rules and not hiding it, with the Garda station only across the road. He could think of no other way. If they sent him home he'd be coming right back.

It was the four o'clock News he had on; he didn't know what he'd do for the rest of the day. There was a stand of trees, off to the right a bit – a minute away. He'd gone in there for a piss on his way back. He'd go over again before he settled down to sleep, in four or five hours, when it was dark.

—At least it's not raining.

There was a man standing near him, beside the car. He had a dog with him, sitting at his left shoe.

He nearly had to remind himself to speak.

—No, he said.

—It's a mess, said the man.

He didn't really look at him. They were both looking out over the water, at the business park and the mountains.

—It's that, alright.

—I shouldn't be out at all, said the man. —I'm supposed to be in, cocooning.

—You're over seventy.

—I am, said the man. —But the dog isn't. The poor lad shouldn't be punished for having a geriatric owner.

—He's a good-looking dog.

—My son owned him but they moved to Perth a year back, so we inherited this poor fella.

—I'm looking for my own son.

—Are you?

—I am.

—Is he long gone?

—Four years. More.

—You've been looking all that time?

—No, he said. —I haven't. I'm only looking now.

—That's what matters.

—I don't know about that.

—Well, I do, said the man. —We all have our stories.

—I suppose we do.

—I know we do. Believe me.

He said no more. He gazed at him, over his glasses. He nodded once, and turned away. He pulled at the dog, to bring him with him. He didn't look back.

The walking was harder the second day. He stayed close to the car for hours till he felt loose enough to move away. He hadn't slept more than an hour at a time. It was just after seven when he opened the car door.

He went the same way, alongside Fairview Park instead of the other way, to the right, through Ballybough. *An Baile Bocht* – the poor town. He'd had children he'd taught from Ballybough; they'd recited the name like they were proud of it. Most of his people had taken the boat to get away from the poverty but the Dubs – they wallowed in it.

He had a feeling. If he followed the same path he'd find something, a clue, if not the boy himself. God, though, he was stiff. The day before was hard, in his legs. This was fear, he thought. Dread – half-molten copper running through his blood and holding him back. He'd just have to carry the weight. His boots were good but the socks were thin; he'd been stupid there – again. They'd have to do. There was no shop open where he could buy good socks or most of the other things he hadn't brought with him.

He was back at the Five Lamps, same as the day before. Again, there was nothing to see, just more of it, somehow. He waited, deliberately waited, then looked up to the right, then turned and looked down the street to the left that went under the railway. There was no one coming, or going the other way. The narrow street right across from him – it was Killarney Street – was empty too. Empty and dark.

He stayed on the far side of Amiens Street as he passed the methadone clinic. There were men and women outside it again. He didn't know if they were the same people, although he thought he could see the woman with the buggy in among them. He kept going.

—Did you find him yet, love?

He stopped.

It was the woman – the same woman.

—No, he called across. —Not yet.

—Hang on.

She shouted something to a man – he couldn't make out what she'd said. He shouted back – he couldn't hear that properly either. She grabbed a plastic bag from under the buggy. The man tried to grab it from her but she pushed him back, and shouted. Two other men held him. From where he stood, it was like a row in a schoolyard or on a football pitch – a load of pushing that was going no further. She stepped onto the street without looking. There was no traffic but, the way she moved, she wasn't a woman who ever looked right or left. He was tempted to turn and get away. She was coming straight at him, frantic in the way she was moving, shoulders bobbing like she was in water. He stayed – he waited the seconds till she came to him, and stopped.

—Hang on, love, she said again.

She looked into the Lidl bag she was carrying. She shook it, then saw what she wanted. She lifted out a plastic bottle and held it out.

—There, she said. —That's for yourself. It'll keep yeh goin'.

At first he thought it was methadone but the bottle, he thought, was too big for that, small though it was.

—It's a smoothie, she said. —I didn't open it. You should prob'bly give it a wipe, but. You never know with this fuckin' thing – the Corona.

She held it in front of him. He took it.

—Thank you.

He could feel her warmth in the plastic.

—D'you've anny wipes? she asked him. —Or the gel?

—I left them in the car.

—They're no good to yeh there, love. Come'ere.

She looked into the bag again, gave it a shake. She put in her hand and took out an even smaller bottle.

—D'yeh have a paper tissue or somethin' on yeh?

He took sheets of toilet paper from his jacket pocket.

—I've this, he said.

—Grand, she said. —Perfect. Hold it out there.

She squirted a dollop of sanitiser onto the paper.

—There, she said. —Now give the bottle a good wipe – go on. And it'll be grand an' safe for yeh.

She put the sanitiser back into the bag as he wiped the bottle.

—Thank you, he said again.

—No bother, she said. —I just seen yeh there. That's me favourite smoothie, tha' one. The mango. Vitamin C an' tha'. Yeh need to keep your energy levels up – what you're doin'.

She'd stepped back onto the street before she'd turned properly and she was darting across, shouting something he couldn't make out. He put the bottle in his pocket.

The bench where he'd seen the men the day before was empty but there were different men – maybe different; he wasn't sure – on different benches. They weren't men he could march up to, show them his picture of the boy. He kept going, the same straight path, up to the station. The morning chill never left him; it was like a slick on his skin. No amount of walking warmed him up.

He went to the kiosk to see if the girl he'd spoken to was there. But it was shut – the grille was down. He looked through a gap in the aluminium slats. The lights were out. The darkness in there – it already had the air of a place that wouldn't be opening again. There was another kiosk open, and the Butler's Chocolate Café place, a long queue outside it because people – not that many of them – were standing two metres apart. It was colder in the station than outside.

There was a van parked where the taxis usually dropped the passengers, and a man was climbing out. An old-fashioned delivery van, it looked like. Deliberately old – vintage. There were drawings of cakes on the van's side and, as he watched the man – a bit younger than himself, but not much – open the doors at the back, he saw wooden trays, like the ones the old bread vans used to have.

—You're working, he said.

—I am, said the man. —I'm one of the lucky ones. Or unlucky.

—Lucky I'd say.

—I'm with you, buddy.

He'd pulled a tray of cakes and buns from a built-in shelf, and he stepped back from the doors of the van. With one hand under the tray and leaning it into his chest, he was able to shut the back doors.

—D'you know what I really like, though? he said.

—What?

—I'm an essential worker, he said. —It's fuckin' great – pardon the French.

—I'd say it is.

He had the tray in both hands now. He'd turned from the van. He'd been talking like a man who was smiling – but he wasn't smiling.

—If I could go back to school now, he said. —For the day, just. There was a teacher in that place – Jesus. Who's the waster now, yeh prick? That's what I'd be saying to him. The cunt – excuse me. You're out and about, yourself.

—I'm looking for my son.

—Oh.

—Yes.

—How long?

—Four years.

—Ah, Jesus. That's rough.

—It is.

—Fuckin' rough. Here.

He lowered the tray.

—Grab a cake there, he said. —I recommend the chocolate mud cake. It'll floor yeh – go on. The ones at the front there. Good man – it has your name on it.

It was a delicate-looking thing. It wouldn't be going into his jacket pocket.

—You're very good, he said.

—We need the oul' treats, said the man. —And come here. The lad you're looking for. I was tha' boy. Are you with me?

—I am.

—And I'm glad my da came lookin' for me. I thank God every day.

He lifted the tray onto his shoulder.

—Keep goin', buddy.

—Thank you.

—Eat the cake there while it's still shiny.

He leaned against the river wall and ate the black chocolate. He licked it off his fingers. He felt full and starving, both. He took out the smoothie, but he put it back in his pocket. He'd enough sugar fighting inside him. He was thinking again of the Dublin girl, the one he imagined was looking after the boy. He wondered if he'd act differently now. If he'd be able to see that she hadn't been trying to hurt him, that she'd been playing – *Duh-blin* – *proved too much for the man*. He'd fallen in love with the girl decades after he'd last seen her. That was the problem. He was no good at living. He was useless. That was the truth of it.

—Why did Mam go?

—Ask her.

—She's not here.

—There you go, so. She's not here. Has she answered your texts? Has she?

—Not yet.

—Not yet – nothing. She won't be answering them. You're not in her plans, boy. Get used to it.


Cruel to be kind. That was the saying. But there'd been no kindness, and no intention of kindness. Only after the boy was gone and staying gone – then he started to think of the things he'd have done differently, the gentler words he'd have spoken.

He pushed himself away from the wall. He got going again. Downriver.


—Mad.

—She is not.

—Bad and mad. And I have it in writing. From the doctor. D'you want to read it yourself?

—What fuckin' doctor? The goofy cunt up the road?

—Stop that.

—What does he know about madness? Or anything? He can't even keep his fuckin' hair combed.

—It was a proper psychiatrist. A top man.

—Only the fuckin' best.

—Just stop it.

—Why should I?

—Mad – like her father. All mad. It's in the blood. Yours too, probably.

—I hope it is – I fuckin' hope it is. I've not much of yours in me anyway, thank fuck. You're not even my father – I've been thinking.

—I am your dad.

—Is that right?

—It is.

—Well, Jesus – all dads are shite, so. Rock solid shite.

—Go find her then.

—I will.

—Off you go. It's no skin off my nose.

—That's not a thing I'd ever want, *Dad*. The skin off your fuckin' nose.

Exhaustion didn't help. He didn't sleep at all. He felt now that he wasn't going to let himself. Common sense – the need to rest, the need to drink water – didn't come into it. He had to punish himself for the lost time. He'd crawl through the town if he had to.

The poor kid.

Why hadn't he let himself think like that – poor kid – back when it mattered? Why hadn't he followed him then? Good riddance. He remembered saying it. He remembered, too, that he'd hated himself when he'd said it. But he'd still said it. And when he'd started to imagine that the boy was safe he'd given him a made-up mother, not his Mam. A seventeen-year-old boy – *There's many emigrated younger, and thrived.*

He wasn't sure now if it was the third or the fourth day. He ran his hand over his chin and guessed by the growth that it was the fourth. He'd shaved before he'd left the house – he remembered that. There was dirt, grit on his palm when he took it from his face. He was walking like an old man. It was what he imagined people saw as he passed – the few he passed. Straightening himself was agony. He'd taken off the boots the night before and had expected to find blood.

There were young lads on bikes now. He'd noticed that. Everywhere he walked. They weren't there the first few days but they were now, there and gone, gangs of them, in black hoodies. Nearly silent on the bikes, two of them on either side of him on the path, passing close to his elbows. They'd the freedom of the streets. Kids, just – they'd no school to go to, mothers at home driven demented. But they looked organised and criminal – sinister. Crows.

He saw a skip, near the canal bridge. On a street off the North Strand. He did a thing that had frightened him, many times: he looked into the skip. He held its side and got up on his toes, and looked. Like he'd done in his mind, many times – the same thing every time. The boy looking up at him. A boy, younger than he'd been. The child, gone feral. Staring, frightened, up at him. Waiting.

There was no boy. Just paint tins and old plaster, and a broken toaster and other old rubbish.

He couldn't breathe. The years, the waste, the badness – they were all in that second, when he looked over the side of the skip.

He sat down on the kerb. He didn't fall. He needed to sit.

He felt the phone pushing into his gut. He took it out. It was dead. He hadn't charged it in the car. He hadn't turned on the engine the night before.

—Are you sad, mister?

It was a girl, a little one, on the other side of the street. She was carrying a red-and-white carton of milk, held in both of her hands.

—I am, he said.

—Why are yeh?

—My son, he said.

—Is he a messer?

—He's missing.

—Ah, is he? she said. —That's desperate.

He looked at her. He smiled.

—It is, he said. —And it's my fault he's missing.

—Well, you won't find him like tha', she said. —Sittin' on your arse.

She wasn't joking, she wasn't grinning.

—Get up out of tha', she said.

The ache in his legs, in his back, hadn't gone. Standing was pain, but he did it as she watched from her side of the street.

—I'm glad I met you, he said. —Do you live near here?

—I'm not tellin'.

—Good, he said. —You're right. I'm going this way.

He pointed at the North Strand, at the block of apartments across the way, one of the city's old cinemas, converted.

—Bye bye, he said.

He could walk again, he could trust himself.

—And mister?

He turned.

—Yes?

—Be nice when you find him, said the girl.

She swam in his eyes.

—I will, he said.

He got back onto the main road. Lads on bikes flew past, some on the path, some on the road. Heading out to Dollymount, he guessed. Be nice, she'd said. That hadn't occurred to him; he'd never thought past the finding. The Five Lamps were ahead of him again. For the fourth, maybe the fifth time – he didn't know.

He'd find him – he would. He'd met good people. The little girl there, the woman outside the methadone clinic, the young girl in the kiosk, the man with the dog, the man with the cakes – people who'd spoken to him. The city was kind. He'd been wrong these years, he'd been wrong all along. He had a day more in him. He'd find the boy.

It was hard to tell the path from the road. There was no real kerb outside the Spar at the Five Lamps, just different-coloured bricks. He had to look down; his feet were heavy. There were no cars or vans, no traffic noise. He stepped onto the road. There was a bicycle wheel at his leg, right against him, and a skid – a shriek, a brake – filled the air a full second after he saw the wheel. He could feel the wheel pressing into him, through the denim – a thin wheel, a racing bike. He looked up from the wheel. There was a young lad, a young man, hands gripping the bars. He'd a black helmet on him; the straps looked like they were holding his beard. He looked at the young man's eyes, then the mouth. He heard the one word – he saw it.

—Dad –?

He put his hand into the jacket pocket and took it out. He'd been carrying it for days; he wasn't sure how many. He held it out – the smoothie.

—That's for you, he said.

# Acknowledgments

My thanks to Lucy Luck, Nick Skidmore, Deirdre Molina, Paul Slovak, Cressida Leyshon, Deborah Treisman, Mary Chamberlain, and Martin Doyle.

penguin.co.uk/vintage